*A*
*Harlequin*
*Romance*

OTHER
*Harlequin Romances*
by FLORA KIDD

# STRANGER
# IN THE GLEN

by

## FLORA KIDD

**HARLEQUIN BOOKS**  TORONTO
WINNIPEG

Original hard cover edition published in 1974
by Mills & Boon Limited

© Flora Kidd 1974

SBN 373-01865-7

Harlequin edition published April 1975

**Printed in Canada**

1865

# CHAPTER ONE

THE winter sun, a round red disc above the dark blue of the distant horizon, lingered a few minutes longer. Then it slipped out of sight and all that was left in the rose-flushed frost-green western sky was the cold sparkle of a planet.

Grass, stiff and rimed with frost, crackled under the feet of a young woman who made her way across a shadowy field. Reaching the dry-stone dyke which separated the field from the narrow winding road, she vaulted over it and began to walk down the hill.

Over the tangle of leafless trees which crowded together in a hollow she could see the long water of the loch shimmering with mysterious light. A ridge of hills, ending in a headland beyond which a ghostly sea moaned and heaved, loomed black against the sky. Over the moorland a golden plover flapped his wings slowly and his mournful cry of *O-dee-ah* seemed to underline the quality of sadness which twilight always lends to a landscape.

It was like a stage setting for a medieval romance, thought Jan Reid, letting fancy have its way. At this time of day when winter's thin blue shadows filled the glen, she half expected the ladies and knights of some story of chivalry to step from the gathering dusk and act out their drama of love and passion. Possibly they would be members of the two clans which had once fought over the possession of the glen and about which many legends were told.

Smiling at her fancies, she paused, tilted her head to one side and listened. Her quick country-trained ears had detected the sound of footsteps. Someone was coming up the hill; someone who was walking with a swing and a

5

swagger, undeterred by the steep slope, and who was whistling a tantalizingly familiar tune.

Who could be coming at this time of the day when most of the local people would be indoors having their evening meal? Only someone coming to visit Tighnacoarach, the Reids' house, would come this way, because beyond that there was no other dwelling except the abandoned croft known as Tigh Uisdean, on which an old cottage still clung to the land in the shadow of the mountain at the head of the glen.

With sunset the air had grown cooler. Jan shivered a little and moved on down the hill intending to meet whoever was coming up at the end of the lane leading to her home. But the whistler was nearer than she had expected and she could see a tall dark shape leaning forward under the weight of the pack on his back. He had passed the end of the lane and was coming on. Where could a solitary walker be going at that time of a winter's night in the Highlands of Scotland?

Jan shivered again, and this time not with cold. The figure coming towards her seemed huge in the twilight. Was it real or was she suffering from hallucinations? The latter were not an uncommon occurrence on a lonely road at dusk and had given rise to the legends and myths often told at *ceilidhs* about the fairies and wee folk.

There was only one way to find out if the walker was real or some giant fantasy created by her imagination. She would speak to him.

'Good evening,' she said. 'Have you come far?'

The walker stopped suddenly. His head jerked up. In the slow-falling dusk it was impossible for Jan to make out the details of his appearance. She had only an impression of height, and of a lean dark face in which eyes glimmered as he glanced down at her warily.

'Far enough,' he answered, and the timbre of his voice was deep and pleasant. He leaned forward a little to peer more closely at her. 'You are real, I hope, and not one of

6

those wee folk I've been hearing about who are supposed to flit about the countryside at twilight?'

Jan laughed, answering instinctively the laughter which threaded his voice. With laughter her confidence returned.

'Ach, and there was I having the same thought about you, only it was a giant I thought I saw striding along. Not many people come this way at night and go past the end of the lane. This road leads nowhere.'

'The road to nowhere,' he repeated slowly. 'But I was told at the pub in the village to come this way if I wanted to reach the empty cottage under the mountain.'

'Do you mean Tigh Uisdean?' asked Jan, and felt the shivery feeling return. No one had lived at Tigh Uisdean for over seventy years and many people thought that the cottage was haunted.

'Yes, I do. Does the name have a meaning in English?'

'It means Hugh's House. It used to belong to a man called Hugh. He emigrated years ago.'

'I'd heard that too,' said the stranger, and for the first time she noticed an alien twang in his voice. 'Do you live near here?'

'At Tighnacoarach, the house of the sheep, down there where you can see the light twinkling,' she replied.

'Sheep!' There was a certain element of scorn in the stranger's voice as if he didn't like sheep very much.

'Yes. My family have been sheep farmers for a long time. We have two hundred acres of arable land and nearly a thousand acres of hill grazing.' Jan was unable to keep the pride from sounding in her voice.

'Some farm,' drawled the stranger with a touch of sarcasm.

Jan felt an unusual surge of antagonism rising within her. Who was he to make fun of the Reids' farm?

'That's quite big for this district,' she retorted spiritedly.

'Not by my standards it isn't,' he replied equably. 'I must be on my way. I'd hoped to reach the cottage before dark.'

'Surely you're not going to stay the night there?' she blurted. Irritated though she had been by his sarcasm she could not let him go on his way without warning him about the state of the cottage.

'I am.'

'But it's almost derelict. There's hardly any roof and the walls are cracking. Grass and weeds are growing through the floors. It's uninhabitable. There's nothing there but an old table.'

He was silent for a few minutes and she guessed he was disconcerted by the information she had just given him.

'You'd best go back to the village and stay the night in the hotel,' she urged practically. 'Come back in the morning to see the cottage.'

'Thanks for the advice. It's not the first I've received tonight,' he replied in cool tones which had the effect of pushing her away. 'Hotels are for those who can afford them. I can't. I'll sleep at Tigh Uisdean.' He made a fair imitation of her pronunciation of the name.

'But how? What will you sleep in? It's already freezing and will be colder later. If you can't afford the hotel I'm sure my mother won't mind giving you a bed for the night.'

'No.' His refusal was curt, almost rude, and was dictated possibly by pride. 'Thank you for the offer,' he added rather belatedly. 'I'll be fine. I'm used to roughing it. I won't be cold, and if I am I can always build a fire. Good night.'

He swung away from her and started up the hill. Hands in the pockets of her quilted anorak, Jan waited for a while, listening to the sound of his retreating footsteps and trying to remember the name of the tune he was whistling.

Suddenly she whirled and began to run downhill, once more beset by the fear that her imagination might have created the stranger. Along the lane she sped towards the distant square of yellow light which was the kitchen window of her home, feeling the ground iron-hard beneath her flying feet. She did not stop until she reached the back door of the sturdy stone house. Hurling herself at the door, she opened it and stepped into the back porch where she paused to recover her breath.

Kicking off her gumboots, she searched for her slippers. Quickly she unzipped her anorak and hung it on a peg beside her mother's old Harris tweed coat and her father's Burberry. Glancing in the small mirror on the wall, she smoothed down her short spiky dark brown hair. Her cheeks were frost-bright and her black-brown eyes sparkled beneath winged dark eyebrows. For a moment she considered her reflection. She was looking much better than she had looked a year ago when she had returned to the glen. Life on the farm suited her. Like anyone else she was happy doing her own thing.

Opening the inner door of the porch, she stepped into the warmth and light of the big living kitchen.

'Is that you, Jan?' her mother's voice called from somewhere in the house.

The table was set for supper. Silver cutlery winked and china crockery shone under the electric light. Near the fire which burned in the hearth an old woman was sitting. She was wearing a printed sleeveless overall over a Shetland jersey and tweed skirt. Her thin grey hair was scraped back from her long-jawed, wrinkle-seamed face. As Jan spoke she turned her head and her faded grey eyes smiled vaguely.

'You are late, *mo chaileag*,' she said in a soft sing-song voice.

'I know, Gran. I met a stranger on the road,' replied Jan, moving towards the fire and stretching her cold hands to its bright warmth.

9

The old lady nodded slowly and rocked back and forth in the sturdy saddle-backed rocking chair in which she was seated.

'I have been seeing him this past hour,' she murmured. 'He is tall and strong and his hair is the colour of jet and his eyes are the colour of periwinkles. He has been coming a long time from a far away place.'

Although she was accustomed to the fact that Agnes Reid, her father's mother, possessed what is known as the second sight, Jan felt her flesh creep a little.

'Ach, Gran, I'll never be able to keep a secret from you,' she teased, covering up her uneasiness. 'He is tall, but I couldn't see the colour of his hair or his eyes. And you missed something. He was whistling a tune. It went like this.'

Jan whistled the few bars she had heard the stranger whistling. Her ear was good and her whistle was strong and true like that of a blackbird. The sound of the tune made her mother, Sheena Reid, pause in the doorway of the kitchen to listen with her head tipped to one side, her brown eyes wide and interested.

'That's *Waltzing Matilda* you're whistling,' she said, when Jan stopped. She went over to the cooker and taking the lid off a pan began to dish up the mutton stew which had been simmering in it. 'I haven't heard it for a long time. Your father had an Australian friend who visited us once. They'd been in the Army together. He used to sing it.'

'I should have recognized it myself,' exclaimed Jan. 'He must be from Australia and that's why he made fun of the size of our farm. They have huge sheep farms out there, don't they?'

'Australia,' crooned the old woman by the fire, her eyes distant and dreamy. 'I mind Davey saying he was going to Australia. "We'll be having our own sheep farm there," he said to your grandfather. "And it will be bigger and better than yours and we won't be coming back here.

Never. Father says so." And he ran off with the tears streaming down his face because he was not wanting to leave the glen.'

'Davey who?' asked Sheena and Jan together, their interest caught by the old woman's ramblings.

'She's talking about Davey MacClachan, son of Hugh MacClachan who used to live at Tigh Uisdean,' said John Reid, who had just come into the room. He was a tall lean man with faded brown hair and the same misty eyes as his mother. He went over to his mother, helped her up from her chair and guided her over to her place at the table before taking his own place.

'I thought you told me once that a tinker lived there,' said Sheena, placing a plate of stew in front of him.

'Hugh MacClachan was a tinker when he came to the glen.'

'But tinkers don't usually have settled homes. They're always on the move,' said Jan, sliding into her chair.

'Just so, just so,' agreed her father. 'Vagabonds they are and always have been, going from place to place doing odd jobs. Usually they bear a good Highland name and can trace their ancestry to the chiefs of the clans. They'll adopt at a moment's notice any trade, provided it promises gain.'

'If he was a tinker how did Hugh MacClachan come to own a croft?' asked Jan.

'Now that's a story your grandmother will be telling better than I can,' said John slowly.

'Aye, so I can, because I remember Hugh MacClachan. Black hair he had and wicked black eyes. Aye, he was a charming rogue, so he was, with a silver tongue in his head. He had only to lift a finger and all the lasses in the neighbourhood came running. But they weren't good enough for Hugh. He had a tinker's pride in his lineage. He saw a way of putting a MacClachan back at Dunmore Castle,' murmured Agnes.

'How did he intend to do that?' asked Jan.

11

'He was after stealing the laird's only daughter. He took her to Glasgow and married her there. When they returned her father would have nothing to do with them, so they went away. A few years later Hugh turned up again. Fiona, his wife, had died giving birth to their second child, which was stillborn. He brought his first child with him, a young boy called Davey, and the old laird let him rent the croft and live there,' replied Agnes.

'Why did they leave and go to Australia?'

'The usual reason. Hugh couldn't make a living on the croft and being a tinker he had the wanderlust in him. He was often in trouble with my grandfather, who told me he once caught Hugh stealing one of his sheep,' said John.

'But we were missing Davey when he went,' sighed Agnes. 'There was no one like him for knowing where to find the first primroses, or where to look for the best gulls' eggs, and he was always good at guggling trout.'

'Good at poaching them too, I shouldn't wonder,' said John dryly. 'And good at telling the tale, like his father.'

'He wasn't all like his father. He was like his mother too,' said Agnes softly. 'He loved the glen and he was crying the day he left. He was a darling boy and everyone loved him. Even the old laird at the castle came to love him, for hadn't he his mother's bonny blue eyes?'

'It sounds to me as if Australia was welcome to the MacClachans if they ever got that far,' said Sheena in her practical way. 'Who was it you heard whistling on the road, Jan?'

'A stranger. He said he was going to spend the night at Tigh Uisdean. I warned him about it and invited him to stay here for the night, but he refused. Gran says she saw him coming. What do you think of that?' said Jan.

'Then maybe she can tell us why he has come,' said Sheena dryly. Being a practical Lowland Scot she hadn't much time for her Highland mother-in-law's second sight.

Agnes slowly shook her head from side to side.

'No, I can't be doing that. It's hidden from me.'

'He's probably one of those climbers on his way to climb Ben Dearg,' asserted Sheena. 'Chris was telling me today that she has a party of them staying at the hotel this week. Now I hope that meeting a stranger on the road hasn't made you forget the tally today, Jan?'

Jan shook her head and told her mother the number of sheep she had counted on the hill that afternoon. She counted them every two or three days throughout the winter, for although they were supposed to come down to the fields near the house where the hay was put out for them, not all of them came, and then a search was on for the missing ones. Many a snowy freezing day Jan had gone with her father and the dogs looking for sheep, fighting the north-west wind as it swept down from the mountains, so cold that it cut through the thickest layer of clothing as if it was only paper.

'That's fine,' said Sheena. 'They're all accounted for and that means we can be off to choir with an easy mind.'

Choir practice was held every Monday night, and as soon as the dishes were washed and put away Jan and her mother set off in Sheena's little Austin to drive to the village on the shores of the sea loch at the foot of the glen.

The practices were always held in a long wooden building known as the Legion Hall. Made up of people not only from the village and farms of Glen Dearg but also from other nearby glens, the choir was conducted by Molly Robertson who taught music at the county high school and was also an organist at the parish church of Glen Dearg.

Tall and slim, of Viking fairness, possessor of a stringent wit, Molly had one overriding ambition, and that was to win the most coveted award for choral singing in Scotland, the Lovat and Tullibardine Shield which was presented every year at the National Mod, that great festival of fellowship and singing which is organized by the Gaelic Society. The shield could only be won by a mixed choir of which fifty per cent of the members were Gaelic-speaking, and Molly, who was a great enthusiast for Gaelic culture and literature, had managed to find the necessary percentage of Gaelic-speaking singers, although she admitted to being two singers short, and still required another soprano and another bass.

Jan, who sang contralto, had been in the chair only six months, but already she was an enthusiastic member and she was looking forward to the trip to Dunoon in September when the Mod would be held. Other singers who had attended Mods on previous years had already whetted her appetite with their tales of the great social gathering; the *ceilidhs* held in hotels; the witty expert adjudication at the competition itself; the glitter of the final concert.

The usual people were at the practice and when it was over Colin Matheson, son of the local veterinary surgeon, who was also a vet himself, came across to talk to Jan. He was a pleasant young man of about twenty-eight who had not long been back in the glen after studying for his degree at Edinburgh and then spending some time working in other parts of the country to gain experience before joining his father's practice. Stockily built, he had brown curly hair and twinkling blue-grey eyes. As usual Jan was pleased to see him, for she had known him many years as he had been a close friend of her sister Ellen.

'I was over at Dunmore today,' he said. 'Andrew Forbes was saying that some of your sheep had strayed into the new forest plantation. He said the fence is down there. You might tell your father, Jan.'

'Yes, I will,' sighed Jan. 'Ach, the trouble we've been having lately keeping everything in good repair. Since Hamish hurt his back we've had no one to do the odd jobs around the farm. I don't suppose you know of anyone looking for work, Colin?'

'Not that sort of work. Everyone around here seems to have his or her hands full without doing odd jobs. Nobody can complain of lack of employment here. The trouble is trying to prevent people from leaving and drifting to the cities. No regrets about coming back here yourself, Jan?'

'None at all. I love it. What about you?'

'Can't think of any place I prefer,' he replied with a grin. 'But perhaps you have to go away from it for a while before being able to appreciate it.'

'Maybe you're right. All the time I was in the hospital in Edinburgh I kept thinking about the hills and the fresh air and longing to be here. I only went there because Mother said it was foolish to waste good schooling on staying at home and being a shepherdess, and because she had been a nurse herself she badly wanted one of her daughters to be one too. Since Chris and Ellen had failed her in that way I was her only hope,' said Jan. 'If I hadn't picked up a 'flu germ which developed into pneumonia and hadn't been sent home to recuperate I might still be there taking temperatures and blood tests, making beds. Ach, it doesn't bear thinking about. Yet Ellen thinks I'm daft for wanting to stay here and herd sheep.'

'Why should she criticize? She's doing her own thing on the stage,' remarked Colin. 'And if I know anything about farming you won't be just herding sheep. You'll be up to your eyes in accounts and records, filling in numerous government forms as well as helping to look after those fine Aberdeen Angus cattle your father is raising.'

'To say nothing of looking after the poultry,' laughed Jan. 'And still Andrew Forbes thinks we have time to mend fences!'

'Well, you have to remember he's only doing his job as factor of the Dunmore estate. He's a wee bit worried about the damage the sheep might do to the new trees which have been planted on that part of the land. He was telling me the Colonel is very keen on re-afforestation.'

'Now that it's fashionable to do it, he is,' said Jan drily, and Colin gave her a surprised yet humorous glance.

'Aha! What's this?' he murmured. 'Do I detect a note of censure in your voice?'

'There was a time when the Langs didn't care what happened to the estate as long as the tenant farmers paid their rents and made a profit out of the sheep. Now that sheep aren't so profitable and there's all this hue and cry about restoring the natural ecology of the district which was destroyed when sheep were introduced, he wants to be in the fashion and to win fame as the laird who restored Dunmore forest to its original state,' she replied.

'Sounds like your father talking, not you,' remarked Colin with a grin as he escorted her out of the Legion Hall.

'Well, I do agree with him at times. He says the lairds of Dunmore have always tended to want the glen to themselves. In the last century the Duncan family who owned the estate then were all for clearing the land of people and trees and filling it with sheep. Now the Langs are all for trees and no sheep nor people either. He's not and never has been very keen on lairds and their like.'

'It's lairds' daughters who get my goat,' muttered Colin in a slightly grimmer mood.

'Oh, you mean Sandra? I haven't seen her for ages, not since she went away to that finishing school in Switzerland. I thought she was going to be married.'

'The emphasis is on the word *was*. She's living at the castle just now and will be staying for a while. I saw her the other day when I was attending to Mrs. Lang's poodle. She looked down her nose at me as usual.'

'But weren't you and she friends at one time? Didn't you used to go sailing with her on the Colonel's yacht down at Oban?'

'Yes, but only because the Colonel needed a good crew member to help him in the races during the Royal Highland Yacht Club regatta. Now that I'm the local vet and own my own racing sloop I'm not considered good enough to associate with dear Sandra,' he replied with unwonted bitterness. Then his open fresh-complexioned face took on its usually cheery expression as Sheena joined them. 'Hello there, Mrs. Reid. Have you found a soprano and bass for Molly yet?'

Sheena, who amongst her many other activities was secretary for the choir, took his question seriously.

'Not yet, but I will. We're on our way to see Chris at the hotel. Would you like to come with us?' she said.

'Not tonight, thanks. I promised Dad I'd be back in time to have a game of chess with him. I'll be over to Tighnacoarach one of these days. See you then, Jan. And don't forget that fence.'

The hotel was a white-painted building at the end of the village and commanded a fine view of the loch where it widened out to join the sea.

'I see Andrew is here,' remarked Sheena, pointing to an estate car parked at the roadside. 'Chris says he often comes down in the evening for a drink. She thinks he really comes to pick up news about Ellen, although he never asks after her.'

'Did you know that he and Ellen had a terrible argument last time she was home?'

'Aye, I did,' sighed Sheena. 'Ach, she's a great worry to me, that lass. I'm not at all happy about the life she leads. I wish she'd get married and settle down.'

'Marriage isn't the answer for everyone, you know, Mother,' Jan objected softly. 'Maybe she doesn't want to give up her career?'

'Career!' exclaimed Sheena scornfully as they entered the hotel. 'Is that what you call it? Not much of one if you ask me, taking small parts in plays. And she always looks as if she doesn't get enough to eat. Ach well, it's no use me worrying. Ellen will gang her own way, like the rest of you, whether I worry or not.'

The entrance hall of the hotel was cluttered with climbers' gear; ropes, rucksacks, pitons and boots. Judging by the sound of voices and laughter coming from the bar the climbers were back from a recent assault on the ramparts of Ben Dearg.

Christina, affectionately known to her family as Chris or Chrissie, was Sheena's eldest daughter and possessed her mother's dark hair and eyes. After training in domestic science and teaching the subject for a few years she had eventually married Gordon Howat, who had trained as a chef, and together they had taken over the proprietorship of the Glen Dearg hotel. Between them they had developed the small country hotel into a popular centre for fishermen and mountaineers.

Sheena and Jan found her sitting in the comfortable lounge of the hotel which was behind the bar, talking to her husband and the tall taciturn factor of the Dunmore estate, Andrew Forbes.

'And how was the choir this evening?' asked Gordon. He was slim and dark and had often been mistaken for his wife's brother, so like her in colouring and build was he.

'We've a long way to go before we reach Mod standards,' replied Sheena, unbuttoning her tweed coat and sitting down in a chintz-covered armchair. 'A wee cup of tea would be welcome, Chris. My throat is parched. I hope I'm not getting a cold. How are you, Andrew?'

'Fine, just fine,' murmured the big man. He had deceptively sleepy hazel eyes which were deep set under heavy eyebrows. That sleepy glance alighted on Jan. 'You've not been over near the estate boundary lately or you'd have noticed that the fence is down near the new plantation,' he remarked.

He always made her feel as if she were totally helpless and incompetent, thought Jan, and the feeling put her on the defensive.

'I'm sorry, Andrew. We're short-handed just now with

Hamish being in hospital. Colin told me about the fence this evening and I'll tell Father about it as soon as I get home,' she replied with a show of coolness she was not feeling. 'I'll come and help you with the tea, Chris,' she added to her sister, and followed her from the room.

In the well-equipped kitchen Jan took out cups and saucers while her sister filled the kettle.

'I always feel as if Andrew disapproves of me,' she muttered.

'He makes me feel the same,' said Chris with a little laugh. 'And Ellen too.'

'Oh?' Jan gave her sister a bright questioning glance. 'Why does he, do you think?'

'He doesn't like independent women. He's a wee bit old-fashioned in his ways. Thinks a woman's place is in the home cuddling her bairns and preparing her man's meals. He doesn't think we're competent to do anything else. I suspect he thinks you shouldn't be herding sheep because that's a *man's* job.'

'What nonsense! Women, shepherds' wives and sheep-farmers' wives, have looked after sheep for ages *and* cuddled their bairns *and* prepared meals ready for their men. Anyone would think there'd never been shepherdesses,' exclaimed Jan spiritedly. 'I suppose it's because he doesn't like her independent attitude that he and Ellen fight when they meet.'

'I suppose it is,' murmured Chris. 'Although neither of them seem to be particularly happy not married to each other.'

'Has he ever proposed to her, do you know?'

'Twice, as far as I know. Last time was at New Year. She refused, as you'd expect. Imagine our Ellen giving up her career on the stage to come and live in the factor's house on the estate! She said herself it would be like being buried alive for someone like her.'

'Yes, I can see that,' said Jan musingly. 'It's funny how you and I like living here in the glen and Ellen doesn't.'

'Well, there has to be a rebel in every family, so they say,' replied Chris with some of her mother's fatalism. Then with a touch of mischief she added, 'Perhaps you should marry Andrew.'

'No! He's too old for me. Anyway, I'm not in the least bit interested in marriage, not for years and years.'

'Not in love with anyone, then?' teased Chris.

'Not I, although there was a house surgeon at the hospital I liked. But when he left and went to Glasgow I didn't miss him one little bit, so I suppose it wasn't love after all,' sighed Jan. 'How can you tell, Chris, when it's love?'

'Ask me another,' retorted Chris with a grin. 'I haven't a clue how you can tell. I just know that it happens.'

A gale of laughter came from the direction of the bar followed by the sound of men's voices in the hallway and the clatter of footsteps on the stairs.

'You seem to have a big party of climbers this time,' remarked Jan.

'Yes, and they're here until Friday, weather permitting.'

'Has one of them asked you the way to Tigh Uisdean?' asked Jan casually.

'No. But there was a stranger in here this afternoon asking for it,' replied Chris. 'He was a tall fellow with a pack on his back. A bit shabby in appearance. His clothes were patched and so was his rucksack and he needed a shave. He bought a pint of beer and asked the way. Have you seen him?'

'I met him as I came off the hill. When he asked you for directions what did he say exactly?'

Chris gave her youngest sister an affectionate yet slightly exasperated glance.

'Was there ever such a curious lass as you are? Ach, I can't remember *exactly* what he said. It involved an empty croft at the foot of a mountain. It was easy to answer because there's only one empty croft around here.

20

Why are you so interested?'

'I don't suppose you asked him his name or where he'd come from?' asked Jan, ignoring the question put to her.

'No, I didn't. I couldn't. He wasn't the sort of person you could question,' said Chris with surprising vehemence.

'Why not?'

'Ach, I don't know. The way he looked at me, coldly.'

'What colour were his eyes?'

'You're worse than a police detective with all these questions,' grumbled Chris as she poured boiling water into the tea-pot and snapped the lid on it. 'Why do you want to know?'

'Gran said she *saw* him coming and that he had black hair and blue eyes. I couldn't see because it was going dark. She'll be so pleased if I can tell her she was right. Was she, Chris?'

'Aye, she was. His hair was black and there was plenty of it, but it was too dark to see his face properly and ...' Chris looked up with a triumphant grin. 'His eyes were blue. The bluest I've ever seen ... like the loch was today. Blue enough to make any girl's heart beat faster if they hadn't been so indifferent. Looked right through me, he did. Any more questions?'

'None that you could answer. I wonder who he is and why he's here?'

'If he stays we'll find out sooner or later,' said Chris. 'And if he doesn't stay he'll be just one more mystery to talk about the next time someone has a *ceilidh* in their house. Here, take the tray into the lounge while I bring the tea-pot.'

The next day the weather changed. Charcoal grey clouds spread across the sky and the wind began to moan in the trees and across the moor.

'Looks like snow,' remarked John Reid to Jan as they

walked to the house in the mid-afternoon. 'The last of winter I hope, then we can start looking forward to spring.'

His prediction was right. The sky grew darker and heavier as the clouds hid the mountains from view. Soon the first few white flakes fell. Faster and faster they came, whirling to the ground. Scenery was blotted out and all Jan could see from the window was a heaving, rolling veil of snow.

It snowed all night and most of the next day. The worst storm of the decade, the news-reader announced on the television before the electric light went out suddenly and the screen became blank.

'Power lines must be down somewhere,' muttered John. 'Out with the oil-lamps and the candles.'

Since power cuts were not unusual Sheena had always kept the old oil lamps cleaned and ready to hand and their mellow light gave the kitchen the atmosphere of another era in time.

'I like it like this,' said Jan as she sat by the fire with her grandmother. 'Electricity is all very well, but its light is harsh. Oil lamps are much more cosy and romantic.'

'Not when you're trying to knit, they aren't,' said Sheena dryly.

'I know what you mean, *mo chaileag*,' said Agnes gently. 'By the light of an oil lamp or a candle a lass's complexion looks smooth and soft, her hair takes on a different sheen. The lines of reality seem to be smoothed away.'

'On the other hand we're also brought face to face with reality,' said Sheena in her sharp way. 'Cows won't milk themselves and if the power isn't back by morning you'll have to be up extra early, Jan, to help milk them. The machines won't work without current.'

'I don't mind,' said Jan, who had always enjoyed the warm intimate moments she had spent milking cows by hand. 'When was electricity first brought to the glen, Gran?

'The old laird Gilbert Duncan arranged for it to be brought to all the farms and crofts, but he died before they had finished putting up the pylons. Aye, he was a sad old man going to his grave without an heir, so to speak.'

'Why didn't he have an heir?'

'He did have one, or he thought he had one. He forgave Hugh MacClachan for running away with Fiona and left everything to Davey, his grandson. But the lawyers couldn't find Davey, so the estate went to Gilbert's sister's son, Cameron Lang.'

'I hadn't realized that the Langs were so closely related to the Duncans,' exclaimed Jan. 'What would happen if one of Davey MacClachan's children or grandchildren turned up? Would they be able to claim the estate?'

'I doubt it. You see, it was willed to Davey, not to them,' said John. 'A thorough search was made for him.'

'Aye, everything was done that could be done,' sighed Agnes. 'Davey was never found.'

When Jan awoke the next morning bright and early to help with the milking the fields and hills were covered in white. In the distance the loch was sapphire blue between white shores. Clumps of pine and spruce added a welcome touch of dark glowing green to the scene and to the north the shoulders and summit of Ben Dearg glittered like crystal shot with rose and gold as they were touched by the rays of the rising sun.

Jan knew that the day would be busy and tiring because every sheep would have to be accounted for. Dressed in her warmest pants with an old Harris tweed coat over her Shetland sweater, a woollen scarf tied round her head and wearing gumboots pulled on over thick fishermen's socks, she set out crook in hand with her father. With them went the two dogs, Flash and Meg, black and white, fleet-footed sheepdogs.

Most of the sheep had come down to the feeding places

near the farm when the snow had started, but a few were missing, including two ewes carrying lambs and near their time. Although April was the month for lambing some ewes dropped their lambs in March, and it was unfortunate that the snow had come because it might mean the loss not only of valuable ewes but their lambs as well.

In spite of the seriousness of the day's work Jan enjoyed being out in the crisp sunny air. There was pleasure in being the first to set foot in the clean snow, to hear it crunch beneath her boots. Many times she paused as she climbed across the face of the moors and looked down the glen to admire the blueness of the loch, the patterns made by snow on the dark conifers. Snow might be a nuisance, but it brought new beauty to the area, giving old friends a fresh aspect.

By early afternoon all the missing ewes had been accounted for except one.

'There's just one place we haven't looked in,' said John, 'and that's the land around Tigh Uisdean. I'll take these two down to the farm while you go through Bealach Glas and search. Take care. I'll leave Flash with you.'

Although she was beginning to feel tired and her feet were icy because several times snow had gone over the tops of her boots and had melted into puddles inside them, Jan set off in the direction of the dry-stone dyke which separated the land belonging to the croft from that of the Reids' farm. Bealach Glas was the Gaelic for Green Gateway, a name given to the gateway in the dyke because in the summer the grass which grew there remained green and thick no matter how many sheep or people went that way.

Today, however, the gateway was not green because snow had blown in a big drift which partially blocked the opening in which no actual gate had hung for years. Jan found a way through and then stood and surveyed the few acres of land. Ahead of her the mountain twinkled with light as the snow on its slopes reflected the rays of the sun. On the lower slopes shadows lay thick and purple in gullies and cracks. In the middle of the field in which she stood was the cottage, Tigh Uisdean, a typical single-storey building with plain square windows set on either side of a plain rectangular door. A smaller building hugged the western wall of the cottage. This was the byre in which the animals had once been kept. Its roof had almost gone and there were slates missing from the cottage roof. One chimney was still standing, the other had crumbled away.

Was it her imagination or could she see a wraith of smoke rising from the good chimney? It was difficult to tell because the snow-covered slope of the mountain soared behind it.

Feeling the wind nipping at her face, Jan moved after the sheepdog as it sniffed at snow-spangled stunted bushes and pawed at clumps of stiff white-rimed grass. The snow was deepest near the wall, so they worked along it, Jan poking with her crook at every drift of snow knowing that each one could contain the missing ewe. Flash sniffed and scratched at every hump and both of them kept their ears cocked for the sound of a sheep's bleat.

It was a long way round and took a long time. The sun slipped lower and the shadows grew longer. Gradually they approached nearer to the cottage and soon Jan could see the peeling whitewash revealing the grey granite blocks of which the house was built. The byre had no door on it, and since no place should be left unsearched she stepped warily into the dark place. There was nothing in there except the remains of an old plough. Cobwebs drooping with dirt festooned the walls and she was glad to back out of it and into the cold air again.

Flash barked on a shrill note of warning and then began to growl threateningly. The door of the house opened and a man appeared in the opening. He was tall and broad-shouldered. His hair was glossy black and needed cutting. His eyes glimmered blue like the loch when he turned to look at her.

Again Flash growled threateningly. Jan called to the dog to sit, which it did reluctantly, its pink tongue lolling out between its jaws, its breath steaming in the cold air.

'Looking for something?' asked the man, and at once Jan recognized the voice of the stranger she had met on the road three days previously. With the coming of the snow she had forgotten about him and was surprised to find he was still in the house.

'We've lost Miss Partington,' she said. Then, seeing an expression of bewilderment flash across his face, she added quickly, 'She's one of our ewes. I called her that after my English teacher at school. I've searched the front field and I've looked in the byre. You're still here, then?'

One of his eyebrows was raised mockingly and a faint smile curved his firm chiselled mouth.

'Well, I'm not anywhere else,' he murmured. 'I met you on the road the other night, didn't I? You're from the farm. You're different from what I expected.'

He was different from what she had expected too. In his early thirties, he possessed an easy self-assurance which made her feel as if she were the stranger in the glen and as if he had lived there all his life.

'What did you expect?' she retorted spiritedly, her black-brown eyes sparkling dangerously. On meeting his cool direct glance she could understand why Chris hadn't been able to ask him questions. In some way the expression in his eyes set her at a distance. There was a haughtiness about him which was as natural to him as the straight set of his shoulders and his proud hawk-like profile.

'Oh, someone a little less juvenile, a plain earnest farmer's wife. Instead I find a pink-cheeked, wide-eyed Bo-Peep, complete with crook and sheepdog,' he replied.

Jan's soft lips tightened ominously and her eyes sparkled even more as she controlled the hot retort which sprang to her mind in reaction to his mockery.

'I'm Jan Reid,' she said, pulling off her thick glove and holding out her hand in her usual frank and friendly manner.

He looked down at her hand and after a slight hesitation took it in one of his. His palm was rough against hers and she guessed he had been doing manual work quite recently, a fact which surprised her because he didn't strike her as being someone who would have to labour for his living.

'My name is Duncan,' he said. Jan waited for him to add another name, but he didn't. Releasing her hand, he pushed both of his for warmth into the pockets of his denim pants. As Chris had said they were much patched, although the turtle-necked blue sweater he was wearing was fairly new and of good quality.

'I'm afraid I haven't seen your ewe. Would you like me to help you search for her? Four acres is quite a lot of ground for you to search alone,' he offered.

A little surprised by the offer, she had no hesitation in accepting it.

'You can come with me if you want to. I've been out all day on the hills and my father and I have accounted for every sheep that was missing except Miss Partington. Father thought she might be up here. The flock often graze this land,' she replied.

His glance was sharp and narrowed.

'I'd thought it might,' he said enigmatically. 'Wait a minute. I'll get my jacket and change into my boots.'

When he reappeared from the cottage, closing the door behind him, he was wearing a thick navy blue duffle coat and a bright red woollen hat which he had pulled on over his dark locks. On his feet were strange-looking boots. Made of tan leather, they were laced and had thick rubber soles. He noticed her curious glance and explained easily.

'The last place in which I worked was Canada. These are known there as "workie" boots and are worn by construction workers there.'

'Ach, and I thought you'd come from Australia,' she said as they set off round the corner of the house to the fields behind it.

'And what made you think that?'

'You were whistling *Waltzing Matilda* as you came up the road the other day.'

'Why shouldn't I whistle it? It's as good a tune as any to walk to,' he replied coolly. 'We'll part company here. I'll search the land to the east of a line going from this post here to the far wall and you take the land to the west. We'll meet at the wall.'

He gave the orders in a crisp decisive way and walked off. Blinking after him in a surprised reaction to the way in which he had taken over the search for the missing ewe, Jan set off in the opposite direction him.

An hour later when the western sky was aflame behind the black hills and the loch was a mere silvery glimmer between dark shores, they met at the boundary wall.

'Any luck?' asked Duncan.

Jan, who was beginning to feel disconsolate about the loss of her favourite ewe, wriggled her toes within her damp boots to try to warm them.

'No, I'm afraid not,' she muttered wearily. 'Thank you for your help.'

'You're welcome.' He touched the top stones of the drystone dyke almost reverently. 'These walls are incredible. Every one of these stones must have been carried and lifted to its place by human hand, and when you think of how many of them there are in this country winding across the open moorland, it makes you realize that the building of them was a labour equal to the building of the great Pyramids, yet I've never heard anyone mention them as being one of the wonders of the world.' He glanced down at her and added in a different voice, mockery taking the place of awe and reverence, 'I've never met a shepherdess before, either.'

His comparison of the old stone dykes which she had accepted as part of her life without question with the amazing Egyptian Pyramids which she had seen only in pictures surprised and alerted her. Here was someone different from the usual run of people she met. Consequently she became wary of him and answered his comment about her own occupation a little stiffly.

'It's not an unusual job for a woman. Most shepherds' wives assist with the lambing, the dipping and the clipping. They look after the hill near the farmhouse where the in-by sheep are kept. They help with the inoculation of lambs and keep the records, so you could say they're shepherdesses too.'

'And do many of their daughters follow in their mothers' footsteps these days when there are so many other distractions?' he asked.

'If they have any sense they do,' she replied with a touch of sharpness. 'Life here in the glen is far more fun than life in the city. There's so much to do.'

'You surprise me,' he murmured. 'Shall we go back to the cottage? It's hardly the weather for standing about.'

She nodded and together they tramped in silence across the darkening fields. At the cottage door he turned to her as he reached out a hand to the latch.

'You look cold,' he commented. 'Would you like to come in and have a cup of tea to warm you up?'

By rights she should have been offering him hospitality, inviting him to come and have supper down at the farm in return for his help. After all, the glen was her home, not his. He was the stranger, yet once again she had the odd feeling that he belonged here far more than she did and was on his home ground, so she found herself accepting his invitation as if she were under some sort of spell and had no control over her own actions any more.

'Yes, please.'

'I hope you won't mind having it in a mug. I don't possess a tea-pot,' he said gravely.

Tea made in a mug. A tinker's brew. Hugh MacClachan who had once lived in this cottage had been a tinker and this stranger was not unlike one with his patched clothes, his thick black hair curling round his ears, his proud hawklike features. He had journeyed here carrying his goods and chattels on his back and had taken shelter in the first empty house he had come to.

Jan followed him into the firelit room which smelt of smoke. Flash slank in after her and lay down in a corner. Duncan closed the door and going straight to the fire stirred it with a stick so that flames shot up, their light painting the grimy walls with an orange glow.

After setting a billycan of water on the fire to boil Duncan walked over to the old table under the window. A match scraped against a box. Its flame flared and was touched to the wick of a solitary candle whose yellow glow illuminated the finely-etched profile of the man who bent over it.

He straightened up and looked at Jan with a smile.

'Welcome to my humble house. I haven't been able to do much to it yet. The weather hasn't been much help.'

'But is it yours?' she blurted suddenly.

'While I can pay the rent for it, yes,' he retorted, his smile fading. 'That's the deal I made with the factor of the estate. He said he'd be glad to see someone living here and working the croft.' He slanted a quizzical glance in her direction. 'What did you think, Bo-Peep?' he jeered softly, 'that I was a squatter? Sorry to disappoint you. I've come by the place honestly, so you needn't think you can turn me out.'

'I wasn't thinking of doing such a thing,' she replied hotly. 'I'm just surprised, that's all. You see, our sheep have been grazing this land for years and the people of the estate have never objected . . .'

'So you've got into the habit of thinking of it as yours,' he put in dryly. 'I suppose that's how your farm has been built up over the years, by taking over unwanted crofts.'

The dryness in his voice made it sound as if the Reids had been committing a heinous crime and roused Jan's pride in all that her family had done in the past to make the farm one of the most successful and prosperous in the area.

'That's true, but only when the crofts had been abandoned for a long time and no young generation of people returned to take them over,' she riposted. 'It's better that the land should be used than left to lie unproductive.'

Leaning against the table, he stared at her where she stood, head held high, her dark eyes sparkling in the candlelight which lent her smooth-skinned oval face new beauty, although Jan herself would never have claimed to possess any beauty at all.

'Let's not quarrel before we have our tea,' he said gently, and again she blinked at him in surprise, realizing that she had been all set to do battle with him and he had spiked her guns by refusing to argue. It was a new experience and she wasn't quite sure how to deal with it.

'Sit down by the fire and get warm,' he urged her, noting her bewilderment. 'I found an old bench in the byre. It's a bit rickety, but will mend. It should support your weight and it's quite clean.'

Sitting on the bench, Jan watched him make the tea. He put a teaspoonful of leaves into each of the mugs, the design of which she recognized. They had been bought at the hardware shop in the village.

He handed a mug full of steaming liquid and offered her milk from a bottle. She added milk to the tea but refused sugar from the package he held out.

Stirring sugar into his own tea, he squatted in front of the fire.

'Is there any work I could do around here?' he asked idly.

'What sort of work can you do?' she asked, not surprised by the question. Crofters often had to take on work to eke out their living and so far he had no animals to care for.

'Anything. Recently I worked on a construction site in Nova Scotia. Before that I was lumberjacking in British Columbia. Before that I was fruit-picking in California and before that I was in Peru . . .'

'And before that you were in Australia,' she put in quickly. He looked at her in surprise, but said nothing.

'You are from Australia, aren't you?' she persisted refusing to be put off by his intimidating stare. No wonder Chris had found it difficult to ask him more questions!

Silence stretched into minutes. She had an impression that he was considering his answer carefully before making it. He sipped some tea, stared at the fire and then said slowly,

'Is it obvious?'

'Well, you have to admit that you don't talk like a Scotsman,' she scoffed. 'You're either a Cockney or an Australian.'

'Sharp as a needle, aren't you?' he retaliated with a grin. 'O.K., mate, you win. I was born in Australia and I grew up there, but I haven't lived there for years.'

'Then what have you been doing?'

'You might say I've been coming here,' he replied enigmatically.

'Why has it taken years to come?'

'It's a long way from New South Wales to a Highland glen,' he replied. 'I had to eat on the way and I had to take work where I could find it. Sometimes I was sidetracked by events and stayed in a place longer than I intended.' His attractive smile appeared, seeming to mock himself. 'In one place I actually considered getting married. Then I suddenly remembered my promise and I re-

32

alized that if I married the girl I'd never get to Scotland. I'd be tied down for the rest of my life. Somehow the prospect of losing my freedom chilled me, so I moved on quickly.'

'But marriage isn't a prison,' she argued.

'Isn't it?' he remarked with a touch of cynicism. 'How do you know? Have you tried it lately?'

'No . . . no.' His challenge confused her, so she covered her confusion by asking another question, 'Why did you leave Australia?'

He finished his tea and set the mug down on the floor. In the glow from the fire she could see that the expression on his face was thoughtful.

'I suppose I was following the trend. Many of the younger generations of Australians like to see the world before settling down. Like the aborigines of that country they do a "walkabout",' he replied casually, too casually, she thought, so that she felt he had evaded the question because the real reason for his leaving Australia was one which he did not wish to be known.

'Why did you chose to come to Scotland?' she challenged.

'Why not? I've always assumed that my forebears came from the Highlands, so I thought I'd come to see the place. I'd often heard about crofts and crofting. When I was in the village I heard there was an empty croft in this glen, so I went to the factor of the Dunmore estate and asked if I could rent it.'

His direct glance challenged her in turn and she looked away at the fire. In its centre there was a long red valley between dark walls of peat, but even as she watched the walls faltered and crumbled and were devoured by the flames.

'I'm wondering how long you'll stay here,' she mused. 'I'm wondering how long it will be before you move on to the next place in your "walkabout". You make me think of a tinker wandering from place to place doing odd jobs.

Did you know that the last man to rent this croft was a tinker?'

'What do you mean, I'm like a tinker? Mending pots and pans is one job I've never done,' he replied easily with a chuckle of amusement.

'They're not always mending pots and pans,' she explained seriously. 'Tinker is the name given to the vagrants who have been wandering about this country ever since the clans were dispersed. They claim to be descended directly from the clan chieftains. They take odd jobs anywhere they can and move on when they run into trouble or responsibility catches up with them.'

'I'm not sure whether to feel complimented or insulted by your comparison of me with them,' he remarked, rising to his feet slowly and looming over her. Behind him his shadow stretched long and black across the floor and up the wall and it quivered slightly in the flickering light. 'I'll stay here as long as it's necessary,' he added quietly. 'Now about a job. Do you know of anything I could work at around here?'

Jan stood up too because his height and breadth made her feel very small and pixie-like.

'No, but my father might. You could be asking him tomorrow if you come down to the farm,' she said rather diffidently, aware that he had withdrawn again behind an invisible barrier.

'I might do that,' he replied politely.

Now she felt that he wanted her to go. He had had enough of Bo-Peep and her curiosity. But she did not want to leave that room which in the flickering light of fire and candle gave an impression of cosiness and security which made her reluctant to face the biting wind outside.

'I'd best be going,' she said. 'Thank you for the tea and for helping me to look for Miss Partington. I'm thinking she's lost for ever, frozen to death in a drift somewhere.'

34

He followed her to the door and opened it for her. The wind blew in, causing the candle to go out. Smoke billowed into the room from the fire. The impression of cosiness was destroyed at once. It was, after all, just a bare uncomfortable room with cracked walls and a broken floor.

'Not to worry,' said Duncan with that touch of elusive mockery in his voice as if he found her amusing. 'Leave it alone and tomorrow it may come home bringing its tail behind it like the sheep in the nursery rhyme. If you don't mind I'll close the door quickly so that I can light my candle again. Good night, Bo-Peep.'

The door closed behind her. She was alone in the night with the chilly wind whipping at her face. Bending her head to the wintry blast, she began to hurry towards Bealach Glas. Only once did she look back. There was a faint yellow glow in one of the windows of the cottage. The stranger had lit his candle again.

# CHAPTER TWO

In contrast to the smoky firelit room at Tigh Uisdean, the kitchen at Tighnacoarach seemed big, over-bright and extremely clean under the glare of the electric lighting which had now been restored. Apologizing for her lateness, Jan hurriedly washed her hands at the sink, then, taking her place at the table, she explained how Duncan had helped her to search for Miss Partington and had invited her into the cottage for a cup of tea.

Her explanation was followed by a rather ominous silence. Glancing warily at her father who continued to eat stolidly as if he had not heard a word she had said, she realized that he wasn't pleased. Another glance this time in the direction of her mother confirmed this suspicion. Sheena, who was sensitive to every mood of her stern husband, was watching him carefully, no doubt preparing herself to intervene should he rebuke his youngest daughter for associating with a complete stranger.

To Jan's surprise it was her grandmother who broke the silence.

'Is he from Australia as you were thinking?' she asked.

'Yes. At least he was born there and lived there, but for the last few years he's been wandering about the world taking jobs where he could find them.'

'Then I can't say I'm liking the sound of him,' said John Reid. 'From what I've been reading and hearing lately there are too many young fellows wandering about the world these days going from country to country unable to settle because they can't take responsibility. A good stint in the Army like my lot had wouldn't do any of them any harm. It would teach them some discipline. He isn't the sort we're needing in the glen. How do we know

36

why he didn't stay in Australia? Did he tell you why he left?'

'No.' Jan tried not to squirm uneasily under her father's sharp glance as she realized that never in a hundred years would someone as set and conservative in his ways as John Reid understand the answer Duncan had given her. 'He just said he wanted to come to Scotland because he assumed his family came from this country and he wanted to see it.'

'He'll be bringing us news of Davey MacClachan,' said Agnes Reid softly.

'I wouldn't count on it, Gran,' replied Jan soothingly, not wanting her grandmother to be disappointed.

'What's his name?' asked Sheena.

'Duncan.'

'Duncan what?'

'I don't know. He just said Duncan. I don't know whether it's his surname or his first name. I didn't like to ask. He has a way of looking at you which puts you off asking too many questions.'

'Aye, I can imagine,' murmured John Reid dryly. 'He won't want us asking questions because he has something to hide that he doesn't want anyone to know. Well, if he doesn't move on in the next day or two I'll be up there to have him out of that cottage. I suppose you didn't think to tell him that he has no right to stay there.'

'But he does have a right,' retorted Jan. 'He's rented it from the estate and intends to live there.'

John Reid's face went slowly red. His eyes grew as hard as marbles. One of his big hands doubled into a fist as he made a supreme effort to control his anger.

'Now, John,' said Sheena soothingly, 'there's no use losing your temper. Remember what the doctor said about your blood pressure and calm down. If the young man has taken over the croft legally he has every right to stay there and to stop our sheep from going on his land.

37

After all, you've been letting them graze there without permission.'

'Turning a blind eye, as Andrew Forbes has been doing over the past few years, is as good as giving permission. And before Andrew came no one else from the estate objected, not even when my father was alive and Cameron Lang was at the castle,' he replied curtly. 'No, I'm thinking that it's all part and parcel of the Colonel's attitude to us farmers and our sheep. Time I had a word with him about who has the rights to the land in this glen.'

'Wait a while, John,' cautioned his wife. 'It will do no good to go rampaging up there and making an enemy of the Colonel.'

'I wasn't thinking of rampaging,' retorted John with a flicker of a smile. 'I was just going to approach him man to man and ask him a few questions and put my own point of view.'

'Aye, I know your man-to-man approach,' remarked Sheena dryly. 'You'd do better to bide your time and wait and see whether the young man's claim to the croft is genuine and whether his intentions are good.'

'That's good advice you're getting from Sheena,' said Agnes gently. 'You'd do well to take it.'

He gave her a sharp sidelong glance. The distant dreamy look was in her eyes as if she was really seeing into the future.

'Very well,' he conceded. 'Did yon fellow Duncan give you any idea of how long he's likely to stay, Jan?'

'For as long as it's necessary, he said.'

'That will be the way of it. He will be staying as long as the glen has need of him,' said Agnes, nodding her head knowingly.

'Sounds to me as if he's clever at dodging the questions,' muttered John. 'Ach, well, as you say I expect we'll be finding out in due course. Meanwhile I hope he won't be doing any harm to anyone.'

'Ach, John Reid, you're that suspicious of anyone who

hasn't a regular job or whose hair is longer than your own or whom you haven't known for over twenty years,' teased Sheena, winking at Jan.

'Any stranger in the glen is an enemy until he's proved he's come in peace,' he replied dourly. 'That was the attitude of our forefathers, and I don't see any point in behaving any differently.'

'Well, I think it's time we did behave differently,' replied Sheena shortly. 'You're always complaining about the glen losing its young people and there being no one left to carry on in the future, but when someone young comes along you want to turn him off because he's taken over some land on which you've had your eye. It's a hypocrite, so you are, passing judgement on a lad before you've met him.'

'And what about you?' he retorted. 'You're accepting him before you've met him. There's only Jan here who has met him. What did you think of him, lass?'

The question confused Jan who had no answer ready. What did she think of Duncan? Her reaction to him had not been at all clear-cut. He had fascinated and repelled her at the same time. She had wanted to like him but had been afraid of liking him.

She hesitated and her father, seeing her confusion, pounced at once.

'You see, Sheena,' he said triumphantly. 'She doesn't know what to make of him, and that's good enough for me. This lad from Australia needs investigating before we let him settle in the glen.'

As usual her father had the last word on the subject and he also changed the direction of the rest of the conversation. The stranger was not mentioned again that evening.

Once again the weather changed and the next day was grey and dank as the wind from the south-west brought a warmer stream of air with it. The snow began to thaw and there was the sound of running water everywhere.

The farmyard deteriorated into a churned-up mess of mud.

In the early afternoon pale sunlight broke through the clouds and the landscape shimmered as every tiny globule of water reflected light. When her work down at the farm was done Jan decided to set out in search of Miss Partington again.

She was just about to leave when a grey car which was well known to her swept into the yard and purred to a stop.

'I hope your mother is at home,' said the woman who stepped out of the driver's seat.

She was tall and slim. Her elegantly coiffured hair was blue-grey and her thin long-nosed face wore an imperious expression. Her well-cut tweeds, her shining brown brogues plus her attitude spelt out landed gentry loudly and clearly. She was Mrs. Hortense Lang, wife of Colonel Lang who owned the Dunmore estate, and she was president of the local branch of the Women's Rural Institute of which Jan's mother was also a member of the executive committee.

'Yes, she is. How are you, Mrs. Lang?' said Jan politely.

'Very well, thank you, dear.' Mrs. Lang smiled thinly. 'You look as if you're about to set off for the hill. I was hoping you'd be at home, because Sandra is with me. She's staying with us for a while and is bored to tears by the bad weather. I thought a chat with you might provide a little diversion for her.'

While Mrs. Lang was talking a tall slim young woman of about twenty-six, whose long red hair swirled about her shoulders, had got out of the car and was coming towards them picking her way daintily through the mud in high-heeled boots of tan leather which matched the colour of her elegant fur-trimmed suede coat.

'Mother says I should know you,' she said to Jan, 'but I keep telling her that it was your sister Ellen I knew when

I used to come down for the holidays. She used to go sailing with Colin Matheson and me down at Oban. Where is she now?'

'In Glasgow. She's with a repertory theatre there. Please come in,' said Jan.

She led them round to the front door and ushered them through the hall and into the stiff unlived-in parlour which smelt of beeswax and indoor plants. After asking the visitors to sit down she went to the kitchen where her mother was baking.

'Mrs. Lang is here. She's wanting to see you. She's brought Sandra with her.'

'Botheration,' muttered Sheena, removing her apron and rinsing her hands at the sink. 'She'll be here to plan the next meeting. We are to have a conducted tour of the castle while she tells us all about the antique furniture she and her husband have collected there.'

'I'd like to go on that trip. I've never been inside the castle,' said Jan. 'I'll finish the baking for you. Shall I put the kettle on too?'

'Yes, please. And get out the best tea-set. Mrs. Lang only likes drinking out of real china, although what difference it makes to the tea I'd not noticed myself,' said Sheena dryly.

Jan removed her outdoor clothing, filled the kettle and plugged it in. Then, using her mother's overall to protect her tweed skirt and fluffy angora sweater, she began to roll out the scone mixture and cut it into small rounds.

The kitchen was quiet save for the ticking of the clock and the flickering of the fire. Agnes Reid was not in her usual place by the fire because she was having her afternoon nap in her bedroom.

As she worked Jan thought about Sandra. The last time she had heard any news about the tall redhead it had concerned the breaking of her engagement to some scion of an aristocratic family. The engagement itself had been announced just about a year ago. A coloured photograph

41

of Sandra which had shown off the silken beauty of her hair had appeared at the time in one of the more exclusive Scottish magazines. A big party had been held at the castle to which many notable people had been invited. Yet now, according to Colin, the engagement which had been greeted with such a fanfare was off.

Absorbed in her thoughts, Jan was startled when someone knocked at the outer door of the porch. Unplugging the kettle, she went into the porch and opened the door.

The stranger from Tigh Uisdean stood there and in his arms was a dirty, bedraggled Miss Partington.

'Where did you find her?' demanded Jan.

'On the other side of the boundary wall, buried under a drift. Searching for shelter she'd run straight into trouble, because as you'll know the snow tends to pile up where there is shelter,' he replied. 'I think she's beginning to thaw out now.' The ewe struggled to free itself from his arms. 'Her legs were so numb when I found her that she couldn't stand. Where shall I take her?'

'You'd better take her to that big shed over there,' said Jan crisply. Seeing him in the soft clear light of the afternoon sun for the first time she realized how formidably handsome he was, and for some reason this made her shy of him so that she hid her shyness under a brusque manner. 'My father should be there. He'll look after her.' Then thinking that perhaps she had been too abrupt she added more warmly, 'Thank you for rescuing her. Perhaps you'd like to come in for a cup of tea and a scone when you've seen Father?'

The blue eyes gazed at her rather blankly and she had an impression that he was going to refuse the invitation.

'The scones are home-made.' To her own surprise she found herself trying to persuade him. 'In fact if I don't go and take them out of the oven now they might burn.'

He smiled and she experienced a queer jolting sensation.

'I'll strike a bargain with you,' he murmured. 'If I'm successful in asking your father for a job I'll come back for that cup of tea. I'm feeling a bit hungry after searching for the ewe.'

He turned away and walked off towards the shed. Jan closed the door and returned to the kitchen, hurrying across to the oven to take out the scones. To her surprise she saw that Sandra was standing by the window watching Duncan walking across the yard.

'Who is he?' asked the redhead.

'Duncan,' replied Jan curtly, as after placing the scones on a wire rack to cool she set about making the tea.

'He reminds me of someone,' said Sandra, letting the lace curtain fall into place. 'Someone I've seen recently, but I can't think where.'

'Perhaps you've seen him in the village. He moved into Tigh Uisdean at the beginning of the week. Or perhaps you've even seen him on the estate. He must have gone to the office to see Andrew Forbes about renting it,' replied Jan.

Sandra drifted over to the table. She had discarded her suede coat to reveal a beautifully cut sage green dress which clung to her shapely figure. A golden chain hung round her neck and a golden bracelet glinted on her wrist. With her dramatic colouring and exquisite clothing she looked completely out of place in the homely farmhouse kitchen.

'Where is Tigh Uisdean?' she asked.

'It's a croft on the estate at the foot of Ben Dearg, just beyond this farm.'

'I'm really none the wiser,' said Sandra with a little laugh. 'Although I've been coming here most of my life I know very little about the district and about the people who live here.' She glanced at the window and said thoughtfully, 'He isn't my idea of a crofter. He looks too

43

... too ... oh, I think the word must be sophisticated, somehow. Don't you think so?'

'He only came here the other day. He's an Australian.'

Sandra's greenish-grey eyes widened.

'Then what is he doing here? Why leave Australia to come here? I'd have thought that there were far more opportunities for a young man in Australia than there are here. I mean, everything has been done here, hasn't it? There's nothing left to do.'

'That's not true,' retorted Jan spiritedly. 'There's plenty to do here. The land always needs to be tilled or grazed. Food is always required.'

'I suppose so,' said Sandra in a bored way, as if she couldn't be bothered to argue. Her glance went to the window again. 'Do you think he'll come back for a cup of tea?'

'He might. It depends entirely on how he and my father are getting on with each other. I've an awful feeling they might strike sparks off each other,' replied Jan as she buttered hot scones and placed them on a plate.

'Your mother sent me in here to ask if the tea is ready,' said Sandra, 'but instead of having it with her and my mother I think I'll stay and have it with you, if you don't mind. Your crofter friend looks interesting and might come back. My father visited Australia a few years ago and has friends out there. Duncan might know them.'

Considering the size of Australia and the fact that Duncan had not lived there for some years it was highly unlikely that he would know any friends of Colonel Lang, thought Jan rather acidly, but she said nothing, thinking it would be more diplomatic to allow the imperious Sandra to find that out for herself.

'No, I don't mind,' she said hospitably as she put finishing touches to the tray. 'Please make yourself at home. I expect our mothers would rather be alone, anyway.

They can talk rural business more easily without us there.'

'They're welcome to discuss it,' drawled Sandra, raising a fine white hand to hide a yawn. 'How Mother can be interested in organizing a bunch of women I'll never understand. Nothing could be more dull, to my mind. Now if there were some men involved that would be different.'

Jan didn't reply, but picking up the tray carried it through to the parlour. The room was looking more cheerful because her mother had set a match to the fire laid in the hearth. Jan stayed for a few moments to reply to questions put to her by the outwardly languid but inwardly alert Mrs. Lang. Then she said that Sandra would be taking her tea in the kitchen.

Mrs. Lang's hard eye softened slightly.

'I'm glad. She's had such an unhappy time lately ever since she and James decided to break off their engagement. I'm afraid the whole business has had quite a shattering effect on her,' she said. 'She's developing rather an inferiority complex where the opposite sex is concerned. Men can often be very callous. Because they find that some girls they meet have very easy morals they expect every other girl to be the same, willing to lower her standard of behaviour just to please them. I'm hoping that a stay in the glen will help her to get over it. I'd like her to join in some of the local activities.'

'Can she sing?' asked Sheena quickly.

'Sing?' The normally imperturbable Mrs. Lang looked temporarily disconcerted. 'I suppose she can. She has quite a good ear and used to play the piano.'

'Soprano?' persisted Sheena.

'Er . . . yes, I think so.'

'Good. Jan and I will take her along to the next meeting of the choir. Molly Robertson needs another soprano for the competition in September at the Mod. This year it will be held at Dunoon.'

'But I thought you had to sing in Gaelic,' exclaimed Mrs. Lang. 'Sandra doesn't know any.'

'A good time for her to learn some, then. Go and ask her, Jan, while you're having tea. I don't suppose you know anyone who can sing bass, Mrs. Lang?'

Jan didn't wait to hear Mrs. Lang's reaction to that question. Chuckling to herself, she made her way back to the kitchen. Her mother was equal to Mrs. Lang when it came to organizing other people, she thought. Imagine Sandra in the choir! Imagine the reaction of the other members of the choir when the well-dressed, super-sophisticated daughter of the laird of Dunmore appeared in the Legion Hall on Monday night.

Of course there was always the possibility that Sandra might think it a bore and not join. Although if she knew that there were some men involved she might be more interested. It was a pity they were nearly all well-married farmers or tradesmen. Unless Colin could be used as bait!

Still chuckling to herself, Jan went into the kitchen and found Sandra back at the window presumably watching for the return of Duncan. The fact that he had not returned yet meant either that her father had sent him off with a flea in his ear or that they had got on better with each other than she had expected.

'Do you like milk in your tea?' she asked Sandra, who having given up on seeing Duncan again had wandered over to the fireplace and had sat down in Agnes's rocking chair.

'No, thanks, nor sugar. I have to think of my figure,' sighed Sandra.

'Why?' asked Jan innocently, taking her own tea and sitting on the chair on the opposite side of the fireplace.

'Because it isn't fashionable to be plump.' Sandra's eyes flickered rather scornfully over Jan's slight square-shouldered figure. 'You should be careful too, because you're short. You shouldn't eat those scones with so much butter. They're terrible for the figure.'

'But I like them and I'm hungry,' retorted Jan. 'Why should I be careful about what I eat? I'm not over-weight and I use every calorie walking the hills and working with the animals.'

'You mean you work here on the farm?' asked Sandra, wide-eyed.

'Yes. What did you think I did?'

'How awful!' exclaimed Sandra, shuddering daintily. 'Don't you ever want to escape and go out into the world and have fun?'

'I tried escaping, as you call it, once and it didn't agree with me. Also I didn't have as much fun in the city as I have here in the glen where life is more natural. Here the air is clear and the water tastes good, free from chlorine.'

The outer porch door opened and there was the sound of men's voices. Immediately Sandra's eyes brightened and she sat up straight, smoothing her hair back behind her ears. She looked with interest at the inner door as it opened.

John Reid strode in. He was speaking over his shoulder to Duncan, who was behind him.

'Come in with you. I daresay you can do with a cup of tea and a scone. If I remember rightly you Aussies are fond of tea, the stronger it is the better. Any tea left in your pot, Jan?'

Jumping to her feet, Jan scanned his face curiously. He seemed in a good humour and he had not sent Duncan packing after all.

'Yes, there's plenty,' she said, going to the table. 'Do you know Sandra, Dad?'

Sandra was also on her feet, coming forward with her hand outstretched gracefully to John Reid in a good imitation of her mother's gracious yet cool behaviour, although her glance was busy with the man who had followed John into the room.

47

'It's a long time since we last met, Mr. Reid,' she said softly. 'I think it was at an agricultural show a few years ago. I was with my father.'

'So it was, so it was,' said John, his rare smile appearing. 'Are you having a wee holiday down here?'

While Sandra was answering Jan watched Duncan. He removed his woollen hat and his dark hair sprang up vigorously as if it had a life of its own. Closing the door, he leaned nonchalantly against it and took his time to return Sandra's quick interested glances with a long cool stare of his own. As she watched them surveying each other Jan could not help thinking that some sort of mutual attraction had sprung up between them and felt a strange little pang of envy.

Then Duncan pushed away from the door and came across to the table. He took the cup and saucer she held out to him in one hand and a proffered scone with the other.

'I was sure there would be sparks flying between you and Dad,' she murmured, under the sound of her father's voice as he talked to Sandra. 'Enough to be setting the barns alight.'

'There were a few,' he admitted with a wry grin. 'But for the time being there's a truce between us. He needs help around the farm, so he's given me a job to do to see if I'm any good. I've to check the fence over by the estate boundary and repair it. The trouble is I'm not sure where that is.'

'I'll show you,' offered Jan impulsively.

'Thanks. If I can do that properly he says he can find more jobs for me to do because it will suit him fine to have a casual worker instead of having to employ someone on a regular basis. In return he'll lend me equipment such as the tractor and plough to help me get Tigh Uisdean into shape. He's even willing to sell me a cow so that I can have my own milk supply.'

Jan nodded. It was the way of the glen. Everyone

helped everyone else and many crofters did other jobs besides working their crofts.

Her father came across for his tea and at the same time introduced Sandra to Duncan. For a moment Sandra looked a little supercilious, then with a smile calculated to win the hardest of hearts she nodded to Duncan and said,

'How do you do? Which part of Australia do you come from?'

'New South Wales.'

'Oh, really? My father visited some acquaintances out there a few years ago. He stayed for a while on a sheep farm owned by a man called Bennett. Maybe you know him?'

'Everyone in the state has heard of the Bennetts,' replied Duncan coolly, and turned to take another scone from the plate and so turned his back on Sandra. He made no effort to continue a conversation with her. Noting the chagrin which darkened Sandra's face Jan decided that it wasn't the first time that Duncan had practised the art of deliberately provoking a woman in order to rouse her interest in himself.

Sheena put her head round the door which led to the hall.

'Your mother is just leaving, Sandra. Has Jan said anything to you about joining the choir?'

'No, I haven't had time,' said Jan hastily, and she explained quickly what would be involved, adding as an afterthought that Colin Matheson had just joined.

This piece of information seemed to have no impression on Sandra and her green-grey glance went again to Duncan's broad-shouldered figure. He was leaning against the table seemingly more interested in scones than in her, and his indifference to her beauty was apparently more than she could endure, because she said to him rather sharply,

49

'Mr. ... er ... Duncan, are you a member of the choir?'

His upward glance was a flash of blue lightning against the darkness of his eyelashes.

'No. I haven't been asked to join,' he replied.

'Ach, you must be the young man who has taken over Tigh Uisdean,' said Sheena, who didn't miss a chance. 'Jan has been telling me about you. Welcome to the glen. I hear that you whistle well. If you can whistle can you sing bass?'

'This is my wife,' said John dryly. 'I'm warning you, she'll not give you a minute's peace until she has you in that choir.'

Duncan's charming smile lit up his face chasing the coolness from it.

'As you guessed, Mrs. Reid, I sing baritone. When did you say the choir meets?'

Sheena's face sparkled with triumph.

'I knew it!' she crowed. 'You look like a baritone. We meet at seven-thirty every Monday night in the Legion Hall. You can come with Jan and me next Monday. Now what about you, Sandra? Are you going to join us?'

With a glance in Duncan's direction Sandra came to a quick decision.

'I'd love to join, but I'm not sure whether my voice is good enough,' she said with becoming modesty.

'It'll be good enough,' asserted Sheena confidently. 'Then we'll see both of you next Monday. I can see it was a good day for me when a stranger came to the glen,' she added, smiling warmly at Duncan. 'Come along now, Sandra, your mother is waiting.'

A little later Jan walked with Duncan across a sodden, snow-girt field towards the head of the glen.

'You are realizing, I suppose, that Sandra would never have agreed to join the choir if she hadn't thought that you might join it too,' she said to him.

'It had occurred to me,' he replied. 'Your mother is a

clever politician. She got two birds with one stone.'

'And Sandra achieved her aim at the same time,' said Jan.

'What is that?' he asked.

'To get to know you better,' she replied, and glanced sideways at him to see how he reacted. He returned her glance and his grin flashed out.

'I'm flattered,' he mocked. 'Who is she, and where does she live?'

'She's the daughter of the owner of Dunmore Estate, Colonel Lang. His father inherited the estate when the old laird died.' Jan paused as a sudden thought struck her. 'That's funny. The name of the family that used to own the estate was Duncan.'

'It's a common enough name amongst people who have Scottish ancestry. Wasn't there once a King Duncan of Scotland?' he replied easily.

'Yes, that's true. He was the one who was murdered by Macbeth. Is Duncan your first name or your surname?'

'Neither,' was the surprising and amused reply.

Jan stopped in her tracks and whirled to look at him, suspecting him of mockery. He was really a most tantalizing person. Obligingly he stopped too and looked down at her.

'Then what is it?' she demanded.

'Just a name I decided to adopt,' he replied casually, although his eyes were frosty, which meant that he did not like her questions.

Perhaps her father was right. The stranger did have something to hide. All sorts of possibilities about him flashed through Jan's mind. Perhaps he was a celebrity wishing to avoid publicity and so he was not using his own name. She did not know the names of many Australian celebrities. In fact the only Australians she knew about were the athletes she had seen on T.V. taking part in Olympic or Commonwealth Games; or the Australian actors and entertainers, seen again on the flickering screen. But she knew that there were other Australians who had made their names in literature and music.

'Did you adopt it because you didn't want anyone to know your real name?'

'Possibly,' he drawled evasively. His breath rose in a little cloud of steam in the cold air. Jan waited, but he added nothing and they stood there facing each other, the curious impulsive young woman and the tough wary man, their figures silhouetted against the background of the sloping snow-covered hillside.

'I know. You've lost your memory,' asserted Jan, who never gave up. After all, the answer to the mystery of Duncan might be as simple as that, and she might be able to help him find his true identity.

'My word, you have a very good imagination,' he scoffed lightly. 'No, I haven't lost my memory. The story is long and complicated and at the moment I prefer to keep it to myself. Can't you accept me as you find me, as an odd job man who has decided to take up crofting in a Highland glen?'

Although the rebuke was phrased politely there was no doubt that he disliked her curiosity. Most of Jan, the young and loving woman, could accept him as she found him, but the slightly primitive inherited part of her, the part handed down from some dark Pictish ancestors who had regarded anyone new and different in their glen as an enemy, was still suspicious of a stranger who possessed only one name.

'It would be easier to accept you if you had two names,' she said, and thought she saw a flicker of relief in his eyes.

'That's easily remedied,' he said. 'How about Duncan Davidson? That's the name I gave to the factor. Will it do?'

He was amused again, playing a game with a young inquisitive acquaintance, and the adult woman in her resented his attitude and longed to retaliate. But she found the name familiar and the reason for its familiarity had to be found. A memory of school flickered through her mind; of learning poems by Robert Burns. She had learned one about a lad called Duncan Davidson. He had had a hard time winning the love of a lass called Meg, but once he had kissed her she had capitulated. Even now the last lines came back to her:

> 'A man may kiss a bonnie lass,
> And ay be welcome back again.'

She realized Duncan was waiting and watching and, although she guessed that the name Davidson was not his surname, she smiled and said,

'Yes, it will do.'

He smiled back and she felt a strong pull of attraction. For all he was a mystery he was tall, dark and handsome, strong with a touch of arrogance in his manner which added to his attraction. She longed to know him better, to offer him friendship without conditions, and for that moment when they smiled at each other the friendship was offered and accepted.

There was no knowing what might have happened next if Jan had not remembered suddenly the way he had looked at Sandra in the kitchen. Her smile faded and was replaced by a frown. She turned away abruptly and started to walk, irritably warning herself. She should know better than to let herself be charmed by a stranger's smile. Duncan Davidson was not what he made out to be and so must be treated cautiously.

He caught up with her, moving beside her with long easy strides, not saying anything. Realizing that her behaviour must seem a little odd to him, she thought she had better try to explain.

'You must not be minding our suspicions of you. It's a hang-over from the past of the glen,' she said. 'Father says that any stranger has always been regarded as an enemy here until he has proved he has come in peace. When you realize that once whole families were massacred by strangers in their midst in the glens it's not surprising our ancestors were suspicious.'

'You mean massacres like the one that happened in Glencoe when the soldiers under the Campbells massacred the MacDonalds?' he exclaimed, and again she wondered at his knowledge of the history of Scotland.

'Yes, although in the case of our glen the trouble happened much earlier than that, and it was not for political reasons. It was just a struggle for land between two clans.'

'Who won?'

'The MacClachans, although they were turned out of their castle and lost their estate when they made the mistake of following Bonnie Prince Charlie. I'm surprised that Father offered you work. He was very angry when I told him you had taken Tigh Uisdean.'

'He made sure I knew he was displeased,' he replied. 'He also gave me a lecture on the inability of my generation to take responsibility, but I think my rescuing Miss Partington proved to him that I've come in peace, and he was also a little mollified when I told him I'd once worked on a sheep station.'

'Was it a big one?' asked Jan, diverted by this piece of information. At least it sounded truthful.

'Several thousand acres and about thirty-six thousand sheep,' he drawled.

Jan gasped, was silent for a moment, then blurted,

'No wonder you think our place is small!'

'Yes, much smaller and very, very different,' he replied coolly, and the coolness set her at a distance, intimating that he was not prepared to tell her more.

'What sort of work did you do there?' persisted Jan, refusing to be put off by that withdrawal.

He didn't answer at once and she thought he was going to snub her by remaining silent.

54

'I did what I'm going to do here – odd jobs. Roust-abouts, they call the odd job men down under.'

After that initial hesitation he had answered smoothly enough, yet she had the impression he was not telling the exact truth. The more she saw of him and talked to him the less she could believe he was merely a vagrant odd job man. On the contrary, he gave the impression of someone who was used to having authority, and his speech was that of an educated person. Would an odd job man know about King Duncan or the Massacre of Glencoe? Would he take such an interest in the building of the stone dykes and compare them to the Pyramids? Jan doubted it very much. Then there was Sandra's remark that he looked familiar. Who was he, and why had he come to the glen?

'What are you thinking, Bo-Peep?' The deep drawling voice startled her. His mocking sidelong glance brought the blood rushing to her cheeks, betraying that her thoughts had been of him. 'Are you imagining perhaps that I'm the son of a wealthy Australian wool king who is travelling the world incognito before returning to take over my father's sheep station?' he scoffed. 'Sorry to disappoint you. I'm no such a person.' Bitterness made his voice temporarily harsh for a moment, but when he spoke again it had gone and the gently tormenting mockery was back. 'I noticed your red-haired friend was a little disappointed too when your father introduced me as his new farm hand. Since her father knows the Bennetts she'll have heard all about wool kings.'

'Well, what can you expect?' retorted Jan. 'How can I do otherwise but imagine when you're so secretive? Wouldn't you rather have me thinking that than thinking you're a spy or a criminal, which is probably the conclusion my father jumped to?'

His laughter was heartwhole and infectious, ringing out over the empty moorland.

'I suppose it depends on the sort of book you read,' he

said. 'If you read romances you create a romantic background for the stranger. If you read thrillers the background is one of espionage or murder. Perhaps I should tell you that I'm neither a spy nor a thief nor a murderer and it will set your mind at rest. I've done nothing violent.'

'Then what are you? I can hardly believe that a roustabout from Australia would know about King Duncan,' she sniped, and he grinned at her tauntingly.

'Does it matter what I've been? Let's forget it, shall we? And you tell me more about Sandra. I've always had a weakness for red hair in a woman. Is she the Colonel's only daughter?'

'Yes, she is,' she replied, stiffening because she felt his interest was not as casual as he pretended.

'Has she any brothers?'

'No.'

'Then she's the heiress to the estate?' he persisted.

This view of Sandra had never occurred to Jan before. Now she saw the lovely red-haired woman as someone attractive not only because she was good-looking and well-dressed, but because she would one day be wealthy and own an estate.

'I suppose she is,' she replied. 'She was engaged to be married, but her fiancé broke it off.'

'Oh.' She was aware of his sharp and sudden interest. 'Who was he?'

'The Honourable James somebody.'

'It fits,' he remarked briefly.

'It fits with what?' she asked, puzzled.

'Fits in with my impression that she's frustrated about something,' he replied enigmatically. 'Is this the fence?'

They had reached the boundary between the Reids' land and that of the Dunmore estate. The land sloped down to a plantation of small conifers, whose snow-dusted clumps of needle looked like so many white tassels

56

stirring under the wind which was sweeping down from the lofty mountain. Through the plantation wound the river which gave the glen its name and, from where they stood looking down, its water seemed inky black against the white shores and they could hear the tinkle of sound made by water rushing over pebbles.

The fence which separated the plantation from the moorland consisted of three strands of barbed wire stretched between posts regularly spaced. Trudging through the snow which had collected thickly in that sheltered place, they followed the fence, searching for a break through which sheep could stray. When they found it they both squatted down to examine the damage. Little pieces of wool caught on some of it fluttered in the wind, evidence that sheep had passed that way.

'Looks as if the wire had been cut,' muttered Duncan. 'Know of anyone who would do that?'

'A poacher, perhaps.'

He slanted her an interested glance.

'Do you get many people poaching these days?'

'There's always someone who'll try to lift a salmon from the river when they think Andrew Forbes and his keepers aren't looking,' replied Jan.

'How do you get on with the factor?' he asked, taking pliers and other tools and a roll of new wire from the canvas bag he had been carrying slung over one shoulder.

'Quite well, usually. I mean, there's no trouble between him and my father, although Andrew and my sister Ellen ...' Jan broke off and he gave her an amused glance.

'More romance?' he scoffed. 'Go on – what about this Andrew and your sister Ellen?'

'We – that is my mother, my eldest sister and I – hoped that one day Andrew would ask Ellen to marry him. Last time she was home he did, and she refused.'

'Why?'

'She's very independent and doesn't like the idea of

having to give up her career as an actress to come and live in the glen.'

'You like living here,' he guessed shrewdly.

'Yes, I do, but I'm different. I wouldn't want to go and live anywhere else. I can understand Ellen very well, though. Why should it always be the woman who gives up what she likes doing to go and live where her husband works? Why can't it be the other way round sometimes?'

'Perhaps it is in some cases,' he replied indifferently, as he began to untwist the broken wire from the posts to which it was attached.

'Could you give up your work and the place where you like living to go and live where the woman you want to marry works and lives?' she challenged.

He gave her one of his lightning-flash glances, blue fire between black lashes.

'It would depend entirely on the woman, and what she had to offer,' he replied curtly. 'She would have to offer a lot. I value my freedom, as I think I've told you before. I couldn't give it up to be at a woman's beck and call. Pass me the wire, please.'

The order was crisp and Jan obeyed it instinctively before she had time to think. When she realized how she reacted, hot words sprang to her lips, but they were left unsaid when she encountered his mocking gaze. He had spoken like a master, politely it was true, but with the crackle of authority in his voice, and she had obeyed as if she were his servant, and now he was amused by her naïvety.

'So there are three Reid sisters as well as a formidable mother,' he remarked as he unrolled new wire. 'Are your sisters as nosy as you are and as organizing as your mother is?'

'We're not nosy and organizing,' she retorted weakly.

'Yes, you are. From the time I met you on the road the other night you've plagued me with questions, and this afternoon your mother organized me into joining the choir.'

'You could have refused.'

'I could, but I thought it might be in my best interests to join,' he replied. 'No wonder your father is a hard man. I expect he has to be like that to hold his own in a houseful of women.' he added derisively.

'Ach, you just wait until you meet my grandmother,' she retorted. 'She saw you coming. She could even tell the colour of your hair and eyes and knew that you had come from far away. She has the second sight. You won't be able to keep your secret from her for very long.'

Even to her own ears her outburst sounded rather childish, but it had a far greater effect on Duncan than she had expected. His hands were suddenly still. He turned and gave her an intent stare.

'What is the second sight?' he asked.

'It's a gift which runs in families. In Gaelic it means literally "two sights" or "two-fold vision". There are two worlds, one of which is visible to those people who have ordinary sight and the other which is visible only to those people gifted with second sight. People who possess two sights claim to see the spirits of the dead visiting this earth and also the doubles or apparitions of the living. Sometimes such people can foretell the future. Gran has a mixture of both.'

'Has anything she foretold ever come true?' he asked in and awed voice.

'Yes. She had glimpses of my mother before my father ever brought her to the glen. Before my brother was killed she saw a funeral procession bearing the coffin of a young person approaching our house.'

'She must be a very uncomfortable person to live with,' he murmured. 'How old is she?'

'Eighty-seven last birthday,' she replied. His glance flicked away from her and she saw him frown as if he were making a quick calculation or possibly doubting her word. 'I expect it all sounds silly to you,' she added.

'Not at all. I'm sure that some people do have powers of premonition to a greater degree than the rest of us, but isn't it possible that your grandmother's vision of me coming here was related to her own hope that someone whom she once knew and who had the same colouring as myself would return one day to the glen.'

It was Jan's turn to be silent as he turned back to the fence and continued with his work. He could be right. From the way her grandmother talked about Davey Mac-Clachan all the time it would be easy to conclude that the old lady had liked Davey very much and had always hoped for his return.

A sad little wind sighed down from the mountain, spraying snow from the trees. Overhead the plover cried mournfully. A few flakes of snow drifted down lazily and were absorbed by the drifts on the ground. It was twilight on an afternoon in late winter when the land seemed to hold its breath in expectancy of spring and the thin shadows listened. As always the silence and the wan wintry light had its effect on Jan as she thought of the boy Davey who had wept because he had not wanted to leave the glen. Was it possible that sometimes his spirit returned to haunt her grandmother?

Duncan worked quickly and methodically. Occasionally anticipating his needs Jan offered him a tool silently and received a nod or a quick smile by way of thanks. Soon she began to feel that she and he had worked together in silent comradeship many times and that he was not a stranger, but someone who was very close to her. The feeling grew stronger. With difficulty she tried to shake it off, concentrating on the small details of reality such as the increasing number of snowflakes whirling down from the leaden sky; the tinkle of water from the river; the plopping sound of snow sliding from the branch of a tree; the shrill sweet sound of Duncan whistling.

He wasn't whistling the cheerful rollicking *Waltzing Matilda* this time, but a wistful lilting tune which she knew well, and in order to prevent herself from being absorbed into that unrealistic feeling of comradeship she began to hum it, hoping that the sound of her own voice would keep her in reality.

At once Duncan stopped whistling to ask,

'Do you know the words?'

'Some of them. It's an old song, but nobody is ever sure who wrote the words. Some say Sir Walter Scott did. Others say that John Galt, the Ayrshire historian, did because he heard it when he visited Canada and heard people who had emigrated from the Highlands and Islands to that country singing it. That's why it's called the Canadian Boat song. Where did you hear it?'

'From an old sheep-shearer I once knew. He'd gone to Australia by way of Canada and other places. I'd be glad if you'd tell me some of the words.'

'I know only the first verse. It goes like this:

> "From the lone shieling of the misty island
>  Mountains divide us and the waste of sea;
> Yet still the blood is strong, the heart is Highland,
>  And we in dreams behold the Hebrides."

It's really very sad when you think of all those people uprooted from their homes here and yearning for the place.'

'Uprooted by sheep,' remarked Duncan rather sardonically. 'His heart was Highland,' he added, and she had the impression that the expression on his face was one of regret.

'Whose heart? The old man's?'

'Yes. He used to talk about the Highlands as if he'd never left them and as if he'd never wanted to leave them.'

'What was his name? Who was he?' demanded Jan,

suddenly excited as she thought of Davey MacClachan again.

'I used to think that he could have been my grandfather,' was the strange reply. 'There, I think the fence is all right now. We'd better start going back. The snow is coming down thickly and I'm not sure of my way on those moors yet. I hope your sense of direction is good.'

Stifling her curiosity which made her long to ask him why he thought the old man could have been his grandfather, Jan climbed up the slope after him. Once they were on the open moor they faced a swirling mass of small flakes which came at them like a swarm of bees stinging their faces and which cut down visibility to a few yards.

'If we can find the dyke we can follow it to Bealach Glas and then we're both almost home,' said Jan. 'Here, hold my hand so that we don't lose each other.'

Holding hands, their heads bent to the onslaught of snow, they floundered across the moor, not talking because to have done so would have meant losing precious breath. Soon the front of their clothing was caked in white and their heads were covered with snow. A dark shape loomed up through the thick grey veil of whirling flakes. Jan stared at it in puzzlement at first. Then as they approached its bulk more closely she was able to make out the glistening wet stone walls of a building, and she felt a certain amount of rueful disgust with herself. She had missed the way and had gone off course. They were at the wrong end of the dyke miles away from Bealach Glas and the snow was coming down more thickly and more heavily than ever.

Quickly she explained to Duncan what had happened and braced herself for some scathing remark. It didn't come. After a few silent moments while they stood staring through the gathering gloom at the building he said calmly,

'What is the building?'

'An old shieling, a shepherd's shelter.'

'How appropriate,' he murmured. 'You're a shepherd-ess and you need shelter, so I suggest we go and stay in it for a while.'

The shieling was nothing but four walls, in one of which there was an open doorway and a roof. It had been built with its back to the north so that the doorway was protected from the blizzard. After being exposed to the blinding snow and biting wind for so long it seemed a haven, rather a smelly one to Jan, and she leaned back against a wall gratefully.

'I'm sorry, Duncan,' she said, 'I was sure I was going in the right direction.'

'Not to worry,' he comforted, leaning beside her and dropping the canvas bag of tools to the floor. 'Anyone could make a mistake in a storm like this. I wouldn't like to be out in it for long. Does it often snow like this?'

'There's always some during the winter. Some years it's worse than others. I remember once a school friend of mine was buried in a drift during a storm when she was just walking from the school bus along the lane to her home. But it doesn't stay long on lower ground because we're too near the sea. This won't last and I'm thinking it will turn to rain before morning. I'm glad all the sheep are down in the fields near the farm. It would be just like some of the ewes to start giving birth to their lambs.'

'In weather like this?' he exclaimed.

'Yes, although April and May are the usual lambing months. Still, tomorrow is called the first day of spring, so we must be prepared to expect anything, and if the cold weather persists into April there won't be much sleep for us because a lamb will freeze to death on the ground if it isn't on its own legs within half an hour of its birth.'

'You seem to know what you're talking about,' he said slowly. 'Seems a hard life for a woman.'

'Only if she isn't used to it. I was born and bred here and I love it.'

'And if any man wants to marry you he'll have to give up his work and take to sheep farming with you, I suppose,' he teased. 'Have you met anyone like that yet?'

'Now who's being nosy?' she riposted.

'All right, mate, I get the message. I'm being too personal. I expect if I stay around here long enough I'll soon learn who has his eye on Jan Reid and is waiting for her to grow up before showing his hand.'

'Ach, to hear you talking you'd think I was a bairn! Waiting for me to grow up! I am grown up. I'm twenty-one.'

'And never been kissed,' he taunted shrewdly.

'How can you tell?' she exclaimed, falling into the trap set by an expert, and he laughed out loud. 'Ach, you're so clever,' she fumed, and tried to move away from him only to find that they were still holding hands and his grasp on her hand tightened.

'Oh no, you don't, mate. I might lose you in the dark,' he cautioned. 'Have you ever been caught out in a storm like this before?'

'Once with my father when I was in my teens. We had to spend the night in a bothy.'

'Do you think we'll have to spend the night here?'

'I hope not,' said Jan fervently, and again he laughed.

'I gather you don't fancy it. Is that because there isn't much comfort here or because you'd have to put up with me for the night?'

'Both,' she asserted grimly, and once more he laughed.

'You're not exactly flattering, Bo-Peep, but your honesty is refreshing and no doubt good for my ego. Still, I think we should consider how much danger is involved in going out into the storm and continuing on our way. I'd hate to end my life in a snowdrift on a Scottish moor.'

'All we need to do is follow the dyke and then we'll be able to see the lights of home.'

'Of your home, you mean. Mine won't be lit.'

He shifted his position slightly and she felt the weight of his arm against hers. He was still holding her hand and in the darkness of the shieling his closeness had an odd effect on her.

'Hey, Bo-Peep? I hope you haven't gone to sleep,' he teased. 'That was reserved for Little Boy Blue.'

'No, I'm not asleep,' she replied stiffly.

'Then tell me which way we should go when we get out of here.'

'The doorway faces south and we want to go east.'

'You're quite sure?'

'Quite sure.'

'I think we'll stay put until there's signs of it decreasing,' he said autocratically. 'I'd suggest that we sit on the floor, if I knew what was on it.'

'Sheep droppings,' she said dryly.

'I thought as much. Are you cold?'

'Not yet,' she replied, and contrarily her teeth chattered audibly.

'Sounds to me as if you are. Lean forward a little.'

'Why?' Again she stiffened.

'So that I can put my arm round you.'

'You don't have to,' she said, and for the life of her she could not keep the sound of panic rising in her voice.

'No, I don't,' he agreed, 'but I'm going to anyway, so that I can keep you warm. Come on now, Jan. You might as well be sensible about this. Shame on you for thinking I had anything else in mind. This is hardly the place for making love. Too damned draughty and uncomfortable. Not a bit romantic, as I'm sure you'll agree.'

'I didn't think –' she began protestingly.

'Yes, you did. Now let me put my arm round you.'

'Very well.' How stiff and prim she sounded! How he must be laughing at her. She could almost hear him telling the tale some time in the future of how he had had to shelter from a blizzard with a staid little Scots girl who

65

had been afraid to let a man put his arm around her. Yet when he did put his arm round her and held her close against his warmth it felt so natural and comfortable that she wondered why she had made a fuss.

They sang to pass the time. It was Duncan's suggestion, and a good one. Jan sang the Gaelic ballads she had learned in the choir and Duncan sang some Australian folk songs about sheep-shearing and other pastoral pursuits as well as one about Ned Kelly, the notorious Australian outlaw. Then they sang together songs that they both knew.

They had been in the shelter almost two hours when they decided they had better look out at the storm. In spite of having cold feet Jan was reluctant to leave the shelter of Duncan's arm. While they had been singing she had rested her head against his shoulder and had felt quite at home there.

Outside the snow had abated a little so that it was possible to see the curve of the land.

'Could we make it now?' asked Duncan.

'I'd like to try. My parents will be worried about us.'

'I was thinking that too,' he murmured. 'I wouldn't like to lose my reputation in one day before I've had a chance to prove myself. Come on, then, we'll go.'

It wasn't easy going along beside the wall, because the snow had drifted against it. As they went the sky slowly cleared. The moon appeared briefly between racing clouds and for a few breathtaking seconds they saw the mountain top glittering with ghostly light.

'A moon to light us on our way,' murmured Duncan. 'More romantic than a smelly shed full of sheep droppings, don't you think?'

Jan was silent, knowing that he was teasing her and didn't mean a word he was saying. He had no romantic interest in a shepherdess who had never been kissed. He probably saved his romantic moments for women with red hair like Sandra.

Glancing down the hill she was glad to see lights flickering; the lights of Tighnacoarach.

'We're nearly there,' she said. 'You'll be coming home with me, Duncan, for a bite of supper? There's always plenty.'

'No, thanks.'

'But you must be cold and hungry and your fire is probably out. You'll have to light another before you can cook anything.'

They had reached Bealach Glas, the Green Gateway, which was piled high with snow. He stopped and released her arm.

'Not tonight,' he said coolly. 'Think you can find your way?'

'Of course I can.' She found herself snapping at him because she was annoyed by his refusal. 'It's more likely you who'll be getting lost because you have no light to guide you. I'd no idea Australians could be so stiff-necked!'

'I'm not stiff-necked,' he retorted, but she heard a surprised lilt in his voice. Her attack had disconcerted him.

'Then why won't you come home with me for supper?'

He didn't reply immediately. In the brief illumination from the moon she had a glimpse of his clear-cut proud profile as he stared past her down the darkened glen. Then he glanced at her and grinned cheekily.

'I'm afraid of your grandmother,' he replied. 'Good night, Jan.'

And turning away he went through the gateway and was swallowed up by the dark shadows.

# CHAPTER THREE

'WELL, were you after mending the fence?'

'Did you not bring Duncan back for a wee bite of supper?'

The two questions, one rapped out by her father, the other lilted by her mother, made Jan laugh as she entered the kitchen. Each was representative of the person who had asked it. One was entirely masculine, showing interest only in the work Duncan had been asked to do. The other was utterly feminine, showing concern only for the welfare of the stranger.

'Yes, we did mend the fence,' she said to her father. 'And yes, I did invite him to come back for supper, but he refused,' she said to her mother.

She noticed that the table was set at one end for two people and she gave her mother a grateful glance as Sheena placed her supper in front of her.

'It was kind of you to think of him, Mum.'

'It can't be any fun returning to an empty cottage and having to cook your own meal on a night like this,' said Sheena briskly. 'Is he shy, do you think?'

'No, he isn't,' replied Jan, and to her consternation her cheeks turned bright pink.

'It took you long enough to get back. Where have you been until now?' asked John Reid, his eyes sharp as he looked at her over the top of his spectacles. With his slippers on he was sitting in his favourite chair and was reading a farming magazine.

'Hadn't you noticed it was snowing tonight?' said Jan with a touch of his own dryness. 'We had to take shelter in the old shieling.'

'Aye, it was a bad wee storm. I'm glad you both had the sense to shelter until it was over,' said Sheena. She was

68

busy knitting a V-necked pullover for Jan with fine natural Shetland wool and her needles flashed and clicked without stopping.

'And I'm hoping yon lad was after behaving himself, there in the dark of the shieling,' said John dourly.

'Wisht now, John! Whatever are you thinking?' objected Sheena. 'This is the twentieth century we're living in and young women like Jan know very well how to take care of themselves. Besides, it's none of your business what a young couple might be doing when you're not there to see.'

'I'm not trusting him yet. There's more to him than meets the eye,' replied John slowly. 'And I don't want Jan getting too fond of him either.'

'I've only known him a few hours,' protested Jan, her face flaming with colour again. 'How could I grow fond of him in that time?'

'Easily enough,' replied her father gravely. 'He's different, a stranger in a strange land. That's enough to attract any lass, especially one like you who hasn't met all that many lads.'

'Ach, 'tis jealous you are, John Reid,' mocked Sheena with a wink at Jan. 'You've been cock of this roost for so long you don't like the idea of a wee bit of competition. He's a handsome lad, so he is. I've always had a weakness for blue eyes and black hair myself. Have you never had any weaknesses yourself, John?'

To Jan's relief her father stopped looking at her and gave her mother an underbrowed glance.

'Aye, I mind I used to have a weakness for red hair in a lass, like yon Sandra's,' he murmured, his eyes twinkling with sudden amusement. 'There was a lass who used to serve tea at the canteen at the anti-aircraft site I served on during the war. I think she married the sergeant. And who was your blue-eyed, black-haired idol?'

Silently admiring her mother's cleverness in diverting her father's attention from herself Jan recalled Duncan saying he liked red hair in a woman and his seemingly casual questions about the heiress to the Dunmore estate. Was it a passing interest on his part, or would he pursue it?

The sound of the telephone interrupted her thoughts and the conversation going on between her parents. Sheena went to answer the summons while John muttered something about it probably being Chris telephoning with some juicy item of village gossip which she couldn't keep to herself until her next meeting with her mother.

But Sheena was back in the kitchen far sooner than either Jan or her father expected. Her face was ashen and her dark eyes were strained with anxiety.

'What is it, lass?' asked John quietly, his eyes alert.

'Ellen,' she blurted. 'She's been burned in a fire at the place where she lives. She's in hospital now. I'll have to go and see her, John.'

Memories of the last time one of their children, their only son, had been in an accident and had never recovered crowded about the couple, ageing them both.

'Aye, aye, so you will, so you will,' murmured John. 'You'd best telephone Chris. Maybe she'll go with you tomorrow.'

'It's a bad time to be leaving the farm, just now. Do you think you can manage, Jan?' asked Sheena anxiously.

'Of course I can,' Jan assured her gently. 'What caused the fire?'

'It happened this afternoon. Ellen was resting at her flat in readiness for the evening performance of the play. She heard screams coming from the next flat and she ran in there to find the place full of smoke and flames. It seems some fat had fallen on the hot-plate on the cooker when the woman who lived there had been cooking and it had set the place ablaze. The woman was in hysterics, crying that her baby was in the bedroom and she couldn't reach the child through the fire. Ellen put a soaked cloth over her mouth and nostrils and went into the room, grabbed the baby and came out. She has first degree burns on her arms and on her . . .' Sheena's voice quavered, then went on, 'Oh, John, my lovely lass, her face is burned!'

The news of the accident, of Ellen's heroism in saving a child's life, swept all thought of the stranger in the glen from their minds. Arrangements were made for Chris to accompany Sheena the next day and they set off in the morning, driven to Oban by Gordon to catch the train to Glasgow.

With her mother's work to do as well as her own Jan had very little spare time, although she found her grand-mother still able to help and willing to do small jobs such as setting the table for a meal.

Two days after the news of the accident Jan was just leaving the house to go and count sheep when she saw Duncan crossing the farm yard. He was wearing new-looking rubber boots, a thick checked woollen shirt with his patched jeans, and he was about to mount the tractor which they used to get about the farm.

Moving quickly in response to an inner surge of delight which she felt on seeing him again, Jan went across to the tractor to speak to him. From his perch on the high seat he looked down at her. Today there was no answering smile, not even the glimmer of mockery on his lean face. The set of his mouth was hard, the tilt of his head was proud and the expression in his eyes was one of anger.

Disconcerted by that anger, Jan could only stammer, 'Where are you going?'

'I'm just off to mend another fence. I guess I'll have to find my own way today,' he drawled coolly.

His oblique reference to their efforts on the day they had been caught in the blizzard alerted her, and a fear that her tactless, outspoken father might have issued a 'hands-off-my-daughter' warning to Duncan flashed into her mind.

'Did my father say anything to you about the other night when we were caught in the storm?' she demanded urgently.

'As a matter of fact he did,' he replied curtly. 'I won't bother you with the details. You must have spun a fine tale to him about what happened. That over-vivid imagination of yours was at work, I suppose. Did he say anything to you?'

Gasping at his suggestion that she had told tales on him to her father, Jan could not speak straight at first.

'Ach, I didn't ... I wouldn't ... How could you think—?' she babbled. Then realizing that she wasn't making sense she flung an answer to his question at him. 'He warned me not to trust you!'

'Then maybe you should be doing as he suggests and staying away from me, now and in the future,' he retorted. He turned on the engine of the tractor. It coughed and spluttered noisily, then settled down to a muffled roar which made it difficult for them to speak to each other without shouting.

Distressed by the misunderstanding caused by her over-cautious, protective father, Jan tried to explain.

'Please try to understand, Duncan,' she appealed loudly. 'He was only trying to protect me because I'm his daughter.'

'Protect you from what?' he shouted back, his mouth curving sardonically. 'I told him he had nothing to worry about and that this year I'm not interested in farmers' daughters or innocent shepherdesses!'

Feeling as if he had actually raised his hand and had slapped her, realizing ruefully that she had only made the situation worse by her attempt to explain, Jan answered rather wildly,

'Ach, I didn't suppose that you were,' she flared. 'Red-haired heiresses are much more in your line!'

His eyes narrowed to glittering blue slits and his sudden grin had a curious saturnine quality.

'Too right, mate,' he scoffed. 'I'm glad that's one message you got straight.'

He released the brake of the tractor and drove it away across the yard and out on to the lane. As near to crying as she had been for some time, Jan watched him go.

All about her the signs of spring seemed to underline the nastiness of the little quarrel. Sunshine was warm and yellow. Birds were carolling in the few trees which protected the farmhouse. In the small garden cared for so lovingly by Sheena the emerald green shoots of hyacinths were showing and swelling. It was a day which invited you to go walking over the hills hand in hand with someone you loved, as Duncan Davidson had done with Meg, in that poem by Robert Burns.

Now a different sound was overlying the drone of the distant tractor; the sound of the engine of another vehicle. Jan brushed the tears from her eyes and at the same time tried to brush the disturbing clash with Duncan from her mind. An estate car appeared and entered the yard, slowly coming to a stop. Andrew Forbes climbed out of it and came towards her.

'Wasn't that the lad who has rented Tigh Uisdean I saw driving the tractor down the lane?' he asked.

'Yes, it was. He's doing a few odd jobs for us, taking Hamish's place.'

He nodded and thrusting a hand into the capacious pocket of his green Harris tweed jacket took out a briar pipe which he placed between his lips without lighting it, and all the time his seemingly sleepy eyes were looking round the farmyard, noting differences since his last visit, not missing any detail.

'That's good,' he murmured round the pipe stem. 'I'm thinking you're going to find him useful. Hamish wasn't working well before his back gave out on him. He's getting too old for the work. I see that the fence is mended and I'd like a word with your father about that to find out if he has any ideas about who's poaching the river. Where will I be finding him?'

'He's on the hill just now,' said Jan, wondering if Andrew ever lit his pipe. She had never seen him smoking it. 'Have you heard about Ellen? She's been badly burned and is in hospital. Mother and Chris are down there visiting her.'

Apart from a tightening of the muscles around his mouth when she mentioned Ellen he showed no reaction to the news.

'Is that so?' was all he said. 'Well, with your mother away you'll be having more work to do, so I won't be keeping you from it.'

He began to walk away from her across the yard to the gate which led to the fields. Jan followed and caught up with him as he was about to open it.

'Andrew, don't you care ... about Ellen being hurt, I mean?' she ventured impulsively.

Instead of opening the gate he leaned his arms on the top bar and still with his empty pipe in his mouth stared across the sloping field dotted with sheep. Seagulls and rooks enjoying the bright windy day soared and sailed on the currents of air, their cries sounding like mocking laughter.

'I'm sorry she's been hurt, but it has nothing to do with me,' said Andrew slowly. 'Ellen chose to plough her own lonely furrow when she decided to go on the stage.' He flicked a glance at Jan, saw the distressed expression on her young vulnerable face; a face which was a gentler, more rounded replica of the face of the woman he had loved and had lost. He touched her shoulder gently. 'Don't worry about it, lass. It's my problem, not yours, and I'll survive.'

'But will Ellen?' murmured Jan, watching the birds gliding down-wind and wishing as she did so often that she could emulate them.

He didn't reply but opened the gate rather noisily and passed through it, pulling it closed after him. Without a glance at her he strode off over the field, a tall silent man, self-contained and unemotional. Too unemotional, decided Jan with a sigh as she turned away from the gate and walked back to the house. Possibly his self-restraint irritated the lively extrovert Ellen and had caused her to turn him down when he had proposed to her. And yet, since opposites are supposed to be attracted to each other and even good for each other, wasn't it also possible that they should be partners in matrimony because their characters were complementary?

'Wasn't that Andrew I saw talking to you in the yard?' asked Agnes Reid as Jan re-entered the kitchen. The old lady was setting out cups and saucers for tea. 'You must be asking him to take a wee *strupach* with us before he goes. And ask the young man from the croft too when he comes back from his work. I'd like fine to meet him and be hearing what he has to say about Australia.'

'Yes, Gran, I will,' replied Jan accommodatingly, although she had a strong feeling that Duncan would refuse any invitation to the house after what her father had said to him. In fact it was a wonder he had agreed to continue to work for John Reid.

Her feeling was right. Duncan did not come in for tea. Nor did he come any other day. He kept his distance from the house as well as from Jan, always having a good reason for refusing the invitations which Agnes issued to him by way of her son.

The week-end passed by in customary activities. Jan went shopping in Oban and on Sunday morning she accompanied her father as usual to the small stone church whose steeple had been a landmark for boats entering the sea loch for many years. Monday came round with its usual routines, and it wasn't until late afternoon that Jan remembered that her mother had offered to give Duncan a lift to the choir practice.

When she mentioned the matter to her father he said,

'I should leave him be. He's an independent body and if he really wants to join the choir he'll be finding his own way there. Your mother always likes to mollycoddle folks just because she can drive a wee car. Yon lad has long legs and he can use them.'

Jan drove down to the village and parked beside the Legion Hall. It was a fine night with a high star-sprinkled sky in which the Milky Way was clearly visible. In the car park she noticed a car she hadn't seen before and she wondered if it belonged to Sandra.

When she entered the hall she saw the smooth silken red hair before she noticed anyone else. Sandra was sitting on the front row of chairs and there was a dark head close to her red one. Duncan, that independent body, had used his long legs, and it looked as if he was wasting no time in getting to know Sandra better.

Stifling a strange uneasiness which she felt on seeing those two heads so close to each other, Jan responded to the usual greetings of friends in the choir, answered questions about Ellen and after taking off her coat sat down between Morag Hunter and Jessie MacIntyre, who also sang contralto. With them she indulged in a fast and furious gossip until Molly arrived, took her place at the front end of the choir, and rapped smartly on her music stand with her baton to command everyone's attention.

Firstly Molly welcomed the newcomers who were asked to name themselves and stand up to show themselves to the rest of the choir. Then amongst wisecracks and laughter she told Sandra and Duncan they would have to be separated and sent Duncan to sit with the basses.

The practice began with the usual exercises in pronouncing Gaelic words followed by the singing of unaccompanied scales. Then the sheet music was handed out and they were just about to start singing when Colin arrived, apologizing for being late and telling them his lateness was due to the fact that a certain prize cow had decided to give birth to her calf at supper time, with complications.

After that all was musical sound, voices lifting and soaring to high notes or lowering and softening to deep ones. Some of it was good and some of it, as the conductor pointed out, at times rather sarcastically, sounded no better than a lot of hens and cockerels clacking and crowing. Time passed quickly and at ten o'clock Molly called a halt.

The choir broke up into groups to collect outdoor clothing and to chatter amiably.

'Who persuaded Sandra to join?' asked Colin, coming over to Jan.

'My mother,' she replied, glancing across the room at Sandra who was making her way over to Duncan. 'At least, she didn't persuade her – she just suggested it and then invited Duncan to join.'

Colin also glanced across at Sandra, noticed Duncan and frowned.

'Do I know him?' he asked.

'He's taken over Tigh Uisdean.'

'Oh, so he's the Aussie I've been hearing about.' He stared curiously at Duncan. 'He looks familiar somehow, and yet I'm sure I haven't met him anywhere.'

'I wish you would try to remember where you might have seen him,' said Jan excitedly. 'There's something mysterious about him.'

'Mysterious or not, he seems to be very popular with the laird's only daughter,' he remarked.

'Yes, I'd noticed that,' said Jan, who had been watching Sandra and Duncan leaving the hall together. She was startled suddenly by the sound of Colin hitting one fist into the palm of his other hand.

'I've got it!' he exclaimed. 'That profile, keen as a

hawk's; his manner – I don't really know how to describe it.'

'As if he's lord of all he surveys?' suggested Jan.

'That's right. Well, it reminds me of a painting I've seen somewhere.'

'Ach, Colin, *think*,' urged Jan impatiently.

'I am thinking,' he muttered, rubbing his furrowed forehead with his fingers. 'I saw it some years ago. It was a painting of a man in eighteenth-century Highland dress. The usual things – kilt, velvet coat, lace ruffles, plaid caught at the shoulder with a huge brooch. He had black hair tied back at the neck. He was handsome enough, but haughty. It was his face I noticed most.'

'Who was he? Can't you remember? Wasn't there a name under the painting?'

'It was just called The Chieftain.'

'The Chieftain of what?'

'I don't know. Of a clan, I suppose. If only I could remember where it was. It wasn't where you'd expect to find a painting like that.' Colin shook his head, then exclaimed, 'It's no use, I can't remember. Let's go along to the hotel and have a drink. It's been a busy day today, so it has. Any lambs on your hill yet?'

'No, thank goodness. I've enough to do just now with Mother being away without the lambing starting, but I expect by this time next week we'll be in the thick of it and we won't be able to come to choir practice for a few weeks.'

Outside the hall they turned to walk to the hotel.

'It's a grand night and there's a feeling of spring in the air,' said Colin, linking an arm through hers. 'About time too. Whoops!'

He pulled her back from the entrance to the car park behind the hall as a car swept out of it. From the light cast by the village's solitary street light it was easy to make out the hawk-like profile they had been recently discussing. Duncan was sitting in the seat next to the driver of the car and it wasn't hard to guess who the driver was as the car roared away in the direction of the glen.

'Nice taste in cars, has our Sandra,' mocked Colin. 'But it's time someone taught her the rules of the road.'

'Why are you so bitter about her? What has she done to you?' asked Jan.

'Am I bitter?' he countered. 'I'm not supposed to be. I'm supposed to have got over it years ago.'

'What was there to get over?'

'Ach, a slight juvenile infatuation on my part for the daughter of the laird. It didn't last long. I was dropped like a stone when her parents started looking higher for a match for their daughter – a title, no less. The local vet's son wasn't good enough.'

'If they reacted like that to you how do you think they're going to react when they learn she's hobnobbing with a stranger who's rented one of their crofts and is a mystery man?' said Jan.

'I'm imagining,' replied Colin. 'And if I know Sandra as well as I think I do after her recent experience with the Honourable James she's ready to lap up any admiration anyone is prepared to hand out to her.'

'Then why don't you try your hand again?' asked Jan as they entered the hotel.

'How do you know I haven't other fish to fry?' he retorted, with a laugh. 'Seriously, though, judging by what I've seen of him tonight the mystery man looks as if he wouldn't let any opportunity pass him by. Also if Sandra's parents offer too much opposition to any friendship she forms with him she might just bolt with him. Their plans for her marriage to a title having come to nothing she'll be preferring to make her own choice from now on.'

Although bothered by Colin's assessment of the situation Jan had no time to worry about Sandra's obvious attraction for Duncan, because the month of April was in and the lambing had started. As during the previous spring she and her father took turns at staying up all night to deal with the numerous confinements which occurred amongst the ewes.

Sheena returned from Glasgow, starting work almost as soon as she had taken her coat off. She had decided that she couldn't be of any help to Ellen and since the hospital would not allow Ellen to return home yet, Sheena had come without her.

'She has to have skin grafting on her cheek,' she explained. 'Ach, she's in a terrible mess, and I'm afraid it means an end to her acting for a while.'

'She can come and live here,' said John.

'Aye, but will she?' sighed Sheena. 'You know how restless she is, and I'm afraid the damage to her face isn't going to help her at all.'

'Ach, do not be saying that, Sheena,' lilted Granny Reid from her corner by the fire. 'It may be a blessing in disguise. Ellen has always been a mite too independent for her own good and being beautiful has not helped her to find happiness. Through this trouble she will be finding her real friends and where love lies.'

'I hope you're right,' said Sheena, shaking her head sadly. 'I'm afraid it's going to take a lot of loving to help Ellen.'

By the end of the week it was noticeable that they were needing assistance with the lambing. Without Hamish, John and Sandra were feeling the effects of having to stay up alternate nights. Eventually, on the suggestion of the practical Sheena, John decided to lower his Highland pride and ask for the help of the stranger in sharing the night shifts.

'Are you feeling you can trust him now?' asked Jan, who was still a little distressed by her father's tactlessness where Duncan was concerned.

John gave her one of his sharp-eyed glances.

'Aye, a little more than I could. You can tell a man's character a wee bit better when you've seen him at work.

This one is not afraid of work, but I can't understand what a lad of his type is doing here. He doesn't fit into that picture he paints of himself as a roustabout in Australia. That Army friend of mine used to tell us about the big sheep stations down under and all about the sheep-shearers, the roustabouts and the jackaroos, and my impression was that most of the roustabouts were rough-and-ready, shy, simple men, slow with words. Now Duncan isn't shy and he isn't simple, and his command of English is that of an educated person. He has an air of authority as if he's more used to giving orders than taking them, and if he doesn't like what you're saying to him he can give you a set-down which leaves you wishing you'd never opened your mouth.'

Jan looked down to hide a grin. It was the first time she'd ever heard her father admit to having been snubbed.

'He was very offended by what you said to him about the time he and I were caught in the storm and sheltered in the shieling,' she murmured.

'Aye, I realize that, but I had to say it, and his reaction told me a lot about him,' he excused himself. 'Now I'm thinking he can be of use to us. He knows more about sheep than he cares to admit, so I've asked him to take over your night shift because I can see you're tired. He says he'll come down tonight about ten o'clock.'

For all that she was tired Jan made sure she was still up when Duncan arrived. He had not been in the house since the day he had brought Miss Partington back, but unfortunately Agnes Reid had gone to bed early complaining of a cold coming on, so there was no chance of her asking him about Davey MacClachan.

As the April night was frosty Jan had made cocoa for them all and her father placed a bottle of whisky and a glass before Duncan as he sat at the table, and told him to take a dram to keep out the cold while he kept watch during the night.

While the two men talked Jan sat quietly sipping her

cocoa and studying Duncan's profile. It was the first occasion she had had to look at him closely since Colin had told her of the stranger's likeness to the painting which he had seen somewhere and which was called simply The Chieftain.

As she stared the sights and sounds of the kitchen faded from her awareness. The high rolled neck of Duncan's white sweater became a fall of white lace at his throat. The dark navy anorak he was wearing became a velvet jacket. Above the white lace the face was long and lean, with high cheekbones and a fresh complexion. The nose curved downwards slightly at the end and the dark eyebrows curved intelligently and rather disdainfully. From the high forehead the crisp black hair was swept back and it was long enough for her to imagine that it was tied back at the nape of the neck in a narrow riband of velvet.

Between thick dark lashes the eyes were blue – not periwinkle blue but the hard glittering blue of sapphires.

Jan blinked and looked again. Duncan had turned his head and was returning her stare coldly.

'Do you think you'll know me next time?' he scoffed.

As she realized that she was alone with him Jan's eyes widened and her creamy-skinned face flushed with pink colour.

'Where's Father?' she asked.

'He's gone to fetch new batteries for the flashlight,' Duncan explained. 'Why were you staring at me? Don't tell me I remind you of someone else, too.'

'Who's said that you remind them of someone?' she demanded.

'Sandra. She's convinced she's met me somewhere else.'

'Has she?' challenged Jan.

'Not to my knowledge she hasn't,' he replied coolly.

'Well, you can tell her next time you see her that Colin Matheson thinks you're like a painting of a man he's seen somewhere, a clan chieftain wearing eighteenth-century Highland dress.'

His eyes opened wide and his eyebrows went up.

'Really? And where can the painting be found?' he drawled.

'He can't remember.'

'Too bad. Who is this Matheson?'

'He's the vet, and he sings in the choir.'

'Oh yes, the fellow who's like a wire-haired terrier. Seems to bristle whenever he sees me,' he murmured mockingly. 'Well, I'm glad the mystery about whom I resemble is sorting itself out. I suppose it proves that I'm running true to type and that my Highland ancestry is showing in my face. I'd like to see that painting. You might let me know when your friend remembers where he's seen it.'

The return of Jan's father to the kitchen put an end to the conversation. Duncan rose to his feet and together the two men left the house.

Jan let out a sigh. She seemed to be no nearer to solving the mystery which surrounded Duncan, although there was the possibility that Sandra had seen the same painting that Colin had and she might be able to remember where it was. But the likeness to a painted face might only mean that Duncan's Highland ancestry showed in his face. It would not necessarily mean that he was descended from the man in the painting, whoever he was.

The brief conversation with Duncan had, however, revealed that he was friendly with Sandra. Would Colin's prediction come true and that friendship develop into something more? Was it possible that Sandra on the rebound from her broken engagement might fall in love with the handsome stranger? Supposing she married Duncan, it would be like history repeating itself. The heiress to the Dunmore estate would marry a penniless crofter who had once been an odd job man, just as Gilbert Duncan's only daughter had married Hugh MacClachan, also a penniless crofter who had once been a tinker.

Jan took her thoughts to bed with her, not liking them, but they did not keep her awake. Nor did she let them bother her during the next few weeks as she worked with Duncan through the lambing season, for being with him in the dark warmth of the lambing shed or out on the cold windy hillside helping to deliver lambs she experienced again that feeling of close comradeship which she had known the day they had mended the fence. Liking the feeling, she closed her mind temporarily to the reality that he was a stranger about whom she knew very few facts, and let the slow spring work its magic on her, tempting her to fall in love for the first time in her life.

But although she was reluctant to see Duncan as a scheming heiress-hunter she had no doubts that he knew a great deal about sheep. One day he diagnosed correctly that one of the ewes, which was having difficulties with its labour, was carrying locked twins, and then proceeded to deliver those twins very skilfully. She challenged him on the matter.

'Where did you learn about that?' she asked.

Blue eyes slanted a wary yet mocking glance at her.

'Oh, I've known that since I was six years old,' he replied, hooking the bone handle of his crook around the neck of one of the twins which had a desire to wander off. Even his handling of the crook was suspect, thought Jan. He was far too skilful with it to have only just learned how to use it.

'How could you know such a thing when you were only six?' she remarked scathingly.

'I saw a picture of twin lambs locked together by their jaws in some kind of textbook on farming,' he drawled, and pushed the twins into the lambing bag which he carried over his shoulder. At once the ewe struggled to its feet and began to nuzzle at the bag. Turning on his heel, Duncan started off over the springy green grass towards the lambing shed and the sickly ewe wobbled after him, as he had known it would, because it realized her babies were in the bag.

Could there ever be anyone more tantalizing? thought Jan, as she hurried after Duncan, too, no better than the ewe. He could have said where he had seen the textbook on farming. No point in asking him, because he would dodge the question somehow and she would end up none the wiser. And did she really want to be any wiser? Wasn't it better to accept Duncan for what he was now — a cheerful, hard-working crofter?

But she couldn't. She had to know more. She had to know why he had come to this particular glen in the Highlands.

'Are you a vet like Colin?' she asked, following him into the shed where he took the lambs out of the bag. Immediately they began to push at the poor ewe, searching instinctively for the food which they knew it should provide.

'No, I'm not.' Crisp and brief, his answer warned her that he was not prepared to tell her more. Together they watched the twin lambs worrying their mother. Then Duncan picked one of them up and handed it to Jan.

'Here, you'll have to look after it,' he said. 'The ewe isn't going to be able to feed both of them.'

'I suppose not. She looks weak,' sighed Jan, taking the small white woolly thing from his gentle hands. 'I don't like having to bottle-feed lambs. It's such a sign of failure.'

'Not this time. The mother is still alive, and it looks as if the lambing on this hill is a hundred per cent successful. We haven't lost a lamb or a ewe so far.'

'It's the first time it's ever happened, I heard my father saying the other day. You've brought us luck, Duncan. Thank you,' she said softly.

'Does that mean you're beginning to trust me?' he queried lightly as they stepped out of the shed into the warm sunshine.

'Yes – although I can't help wishing you'd tell us more about yourself.'

'There's nothing to tell,' he replied curtly. 'My life started when I took over Tigh Uisdean.'

'Ach, how can you say that when I know you had a life in Australia and in all those other places you've worked in?' she admonished him. 'You want us to trust you, but you won't trust us. If you did trust me you'd be willing to answer my questions instead of dodging them. Why won't you trust me, Duncan?'

She raised appealing black-brown eyes to look at him. He returned her gaze coolly, although a muscle twitched at the corner of his mouth and he seemed to lose a little colour as he refused to be moved by that appeal.

'Because you ask too many questions and I don't like being quizzed,' he drawled. 'That's all there is to it. Stop asking questions and you'll find that you and I will get along fine together. Continue to ask them and I'll be forced to silence you in the only effective way I know for dealing with an inquisitive woman.'

There was a threatening glint in his eyes and for a moment she stood her ground, seriously thinking of challenging him by asking another question just to see how he would silence her. But the sound of her mother's voice calling to her from the house reminded her that there was other work to do and that she had no more time for dallying on the hillside with an attractive stranger even though the spring sunshine was tempting her to do so.

'All right,' she said in a low voice. 'You win today. I won't be asking you any more questions, but you can't stop me from thinking them – or from trying to find answers to them!'

Pleased with her retort, she turned, and still cuddling the lamb, walked away to the house.

Within a few days the lambing season was over for another year. It had been the most successful season John

Reid had ever known and he was inclined to attribute the success to having had Duncan's help, and consequently his attitude to the stranger changed.

'It's a fine shepherd you are,' he said. 'I'm hoping you will give us a hand at clipping time. There are a few other jobs I have in mind, too.'

'I'll help you when I can, but not tomorrow or next week. I have to see to my own place.'

'Aye, that's so. You can have the use of the plough and tractor and any advice I can be giving you about which crops you should sow.'

'Thank you,' said Duncan. 'Where would be the best place for buying wood? I still have some repairs to do to the cottage.'

'I'm thinking you'd best go into Oban,' replied John. 'A bus leaves the village at ten in the morning. You could be taking it.'

Once more Duncan thanked him and walked away through the yard on his way back to the croft.

In the house Sheena was busy with the end of the month accounts and immediately she wanted to know if Duncan would be coming to do more work about the farm. John told her the answer and mentioned that Duncan would be going to Oban.

'What good is a bus when you're wanting to buy timber and bring it back here?' exclaimed the practical Sheena. 'Jan has to go into the town tomorrow for me. They could go together in the Land-Rover. It's the least we can do to help him after his hard work on the hill these past weeks. Run after him now, lass, and tell him you'll give him a lift there and back.'

Out in the farmyard the slanting rays of the westering sun gilded the walls of sheds and barns. The shadows of bent pine trees and old gates were black against the bleached grass of the hillside. Here and there a new lamb bleated plaintively and overhead the inevitable plover flapped his wings as he hovered over the moor guarding his broody hen who was sitting on her eggs in some tussock.

Jan didn't catch up with Duncan until she reached Bealach Glas, where he had paused to inspect the patch of grass which was already turning green. She told him of her mother's suggestion. He did not answer at once and sensing that he was reluctant to commit himself she felt a sudden nagging disappointment, then inwardly berated herself. Why should she hope that he would go with her? He'd probably had enough of her during the past three weeks.

'Would you like me to go with you?' he asked slowly, glancing at her, and the question took her by surprise, showing as it did his consideration for her feelings.

'I . . . I . . .' Jan stammered, and stopped.

'I don't want you to think you have to give me a lift just because your mother says you have to. I'm quite capable of going on the bus,' he said.

'No, I'd like you to come with me. I mean, I'm not offering to take you because she says so. Ach, Duncan, you're a terrible tease. What do you want me to say?' she exclaimed as she noted a glimmer of laughter in his eyes.

'Only what you feel. Don't ask me to go with you just because someone else says you should.'

'I'm not doing that at all. It's you who are so stiff-necked. You just hate accepting offers of help,' she retorted. 'You're very welcome to come with me. You can even drive, that is if you have a licence.'

'Since you put it that way – O.K., mate, I'll come with you, I have a licence. What time?'

He was smiling now and Jan's spirits soared ridiculously as if they had some reason for doing so. The still April evening seemed to be suddenly enchanted and the glen a serene and smiling place. She told him a time and he nodded, then turned his attention once more to the grass beneath their feet.

'Why is it greener than the other grass?' he asked.

'I believe it's because there's an underground spring of water, something to do with this hill being a limestone outcrop,' she said. 'Although my grandmother has another explanation.'

Interest flashed in his eyes as he looked up.

'What is that? Something to do with fairies and elves, I'll bet,' he murmured.

'Yes. She says that it's the fairies who keep the grass soft and green for lovers to lie on in the summer,' replied Jan, glancing away from that derisive blue glance, down to the distant loch which was beginning to disappear under a pale mist.

'But do any lovers ever come this way?' he asked.

'Not now, but Gran says that when she was a girl, working for the Reids, my great-grandmother sent her after my grandfather who had forgotten to take his luncheon basket. It was a lovely sunny day and she caught up with him at this gateway . . .' Jan's voice died away as she realized what she was saying. She had been sent after Duncan and had caught up with him at exactly the same place.

'Go on,' he urged. 'What happened then?'

'They sat on the grass and shared his lunch,' said Jan in a flat matter-of-fact voice.

'And lived happily ever after,' he mocked. 'I'm sure your grandmother tells it better than that.'

'Then why don't you come and ask her yourself?' she sniped.

'Maybe I will, one day,' he replied equably. 'See you tomorrow.'

The enchantment she had felt for those few moments as she had stood with Duncan at Bealach Glas returned the next morning when they set out for Oban. It was the first of May when according to the traditions of this northern land the farm animals were taken from the byres in which they had been kept all winter and were put out into the fields to graze. In days gone by the fires of Beltane had blazed from the hilltops and around those fires young couples had danced to celebrate the end of winter and the coming of summer; or had sat together in the twilight dreaming and planning for the future.

Something of that May Day spirit bubbled up in Jan as she sat beside Duncan in the Land-Rover and they bumped down the glen road to the village. It seemed to her that they were both celebrating by going out for the day to Oban.

Everything looked brighter and fresher than ever before. Ben Dearg's summit sparkled like crystal. The river, in full spate from the melting of snows, glittered and babbled in its rocky bed. Down by the loch-side the neat white houses of the village admired their swaying reflections in the water and beyond the dark headlands the sea shimmered with golden light.

Once off the ferry which took them across to the other side of the loch the Land-Rover roared up the steep slope and then took the road which curved through Dunmore forest. Silvery barks of birches gleamed against the dark background of pine and spruce. Rhododendron buds, thick and pointed, were ready to burst into purple, rose and violet-coloured blossoms.

As they passed the huge stone gateposts which guarded the entrance to the castle driveway Jan noticed Duncan's curious sidelong glance at them and wondered if he had noticed, as she had, the car which was waiting for the traffic from the ferry to pass before it moved out into the road. Sandra's car. Which way would she be going? To the village? Or to Oban?

The gloom of the forest was left behind and the road ran beside the loch again on the opposite side from the village. On the narrow rim of shingle beach Jan could see flashes of black and white as oyster-catchers searched for shell fish. Out over the blue water Arctic terns swooped and pirouetted in a perpetual ballet dance.

Eventually the road curved away from the glitter of water and crossed a wide neck of flat fertile land which was scattered with white cottages. Brown and white cattle, let out only that morning, were cropping at new grass and behind them across another stretch of water mountains reared up, purple black against the sun-bright sky; the mountains of the island of Mull.

Jan pointed them out to Duncan.

'At last I behold a Hebridean island,' he murmured. 'And I'm glad to say it isn't in my dreams.'

She gave him a curious glance, but did not question him as she was tempted to do. Today would be a day without any questions on her part. She would forget he was a stranger who was reluctant to reveal his past and would enjoy being with him no matter what the consequences might be.

Oban, built on the shores of a wide natural bay, famed for its fishing fleet and its sunsets, seemed to sparkle in the May sunshine. On a hill behind the main part of the town McCaig's Folly, a circular building with some resemblance to the Colosseum, gave a strangely Roman air to the town whose buildings were mostly a typical blend of simple straight-sided, high-shouldered, plain-fronted Scottish houses and the more ornately-gabled villas and hotels which had been built in Victorian and Edwardian times.

Since Duncan had said he had recently received a cheque which he wanted to cash they went straight to the bank where the Reids normally did their financial transactions, where Jan introduced him to the teller. Once that was done they went out into the sunshine again and stood for a while admiring the view across the rippling water to the green island of Kerrera.

'Now where shall we go?' asked Jan.

'A timber yard, then a hardware store for me. I need screws and paint. I could also do with some slates for the roof,' said Duncan.

'You'd best be having the help of Alec MacKinnon for the roof. He's the best slater in the glen,' replied Jan.

'I can see I should have consulted you before,' he said with a grin. 'All right, no slates, but timber I must have.'

She took him to a timber yard. The discussion about what he needed with the proprietor, who was another friend of John Reid, took a long time because there was no hurry on that lovely bright morning, and by the time they left the yard with the lengths of timber loaded in the back of the vehicle it was almost midday. Mindful that she had to shop for her mother, Jan left Duncan in a hardware shop while she visited a drapers to buy the wool and sewing things which Sheena required. When she returned to the hardware shop she found Duncan waiting for her laden with packages and tins of paint. When they had loaded everything into the Land-Rover Jan asked,

'What now?'

'Food. Haggling makes me hungry. The best this place can offer.'

She named a hotel on the sea-front and they walked along the Corran Esplanade where seagulls glided and cried, swept in from the sea by the steady westerly breeze which tossed Jan's shining hair and twitched at her pleated skirt.

In the entrance hall of the old established hotel Jan half expected the commissionaire to turn them away when he gave a disdainful glance at Duncan's casual clothing – white roll-necked sweater, rather shabby grey trousers and scuffed navy blue anorak. But when his glance came up to the haughty profile he almost bowed.

'Luncheon, sir? In the dining-room, first on the left,' he murmured deferentially, and Jan was almost laughing at his change of attitude.

The hallway was just the same as it had always been, she thought. Sunlight slanted across the shining polished floors and glinted on the heavy gilt frames of the pictures of sailing ships which hung on the walls. From a room on the left came the drone of voices as people conversed over their meal. The droning stopped for a few moments when she and Duncan entered and she guessed they were eyeing covertly the stranger whose profile might seem vaguely familiar but whose height, breadth and clothing implied that he was not a local.

They sat at a table for two near a window from which they could see the sunlight twinkling on the waters of the Sound and the mountains of Mull which were now a hazy blue in the afternoon sun.

Throughout the meal the magic held, and if anyone had asked Jan in after years what she and Duncan talked about or what they ate that day, she could not have told them. It was the mood she remembered. For a brief hour she experienced a happiness which she had not known before.

It came to an end all too soon. The bill was presented, Duncan picked it up and glanced at it, but when Jan asked him the amount of her share, he said,

'This is my treat.'

'No. I can pay for myself,' she asserted independently.

'Now who's being stiff-necked?' he teased. 'You won't pay for yourself, because I won't let you. I've just received the first cheque I've had in three months and I'm on the spree today with the prettiest shepherdess in the whole of the Highlands.'

Although she was delighted to find that his mood corresponded with hers Jan couldn't help wondering where his cheque had come from, but she suppressed her curiosity again, wishing she could control the blush which stole into her cheeks in reaction to his compliment.

'Very well,' she agreed sedately. 'You can pay for the meal, but you don't have to say I'm pretty.'

'Why not? I think you are pretty and I'm saying so.

Hasn't anyone ever told you that when you laugh your eyes sparkle and that your cheeks glow like sun-kissed peaches?' he asked softly.

Her head was whirling. Shaking it a little, she glanced at him warily. He was watching her gravely, his eyes as blue as the twinkling water of the bay which she could see through the window.

'You must know that no one has ever talked such non-sense to me,' she replied.

'Not even the wire-haired terrier?' he inquired with a humorous twitch of his mouth. 'I mean the amiable vet.'

'No, of course he hasn't. Why should he?'

'Why shouldn't he?' he countered. 'He's the one who's waiting for you to grow up, isn't he?'

She was so astonished that she could only stare at him, her dark eyes round. Colin waiting for her to grow up so that he could marry her? The whole idea was ridiculous – until she remembered Colin himself saying that he had other fish than Sandra to fry.

'Where did you get that idea?' she gasped at last.

'I have eyes to see with, and I've seen you with him at choir practice and when he's visited the farm. He's very chummy with you.'

'Why shouldn't he be? I've known him for years, ever since I was a child, but I've never had reason to think he might be waiting for me to grow up so that he can marry me,' she defended.

'But isn't that how it goes sometimes?' he murmured. 'You know a person for years and years, but you never really notice him or her. Then one day someone or some-thing wakes you up. Perhaps it needed a stranger like me coming into your life to jolt you into awareness. I notice more about the people in the glen than you because it's all new to me.'

It could be true, she thought, remembering the times Colin had sought her out lately after choir practice; the times he had called at the farm when there was no reason for him to do so; the odd little invitations he issued and which she sometimes accepted. Thus might a shy Scotsman do his courting.

'But if he's waiting I must tell him not to,' she muttered, speaking a thought aloud.

'Why, aren't you going to grow up after all?' Duncan teased lazily.

'I'm grown up,' she flashed, 'but I'm not sure I want to marry Colin.'

'He seems highly eligible to me,' he drawled. 'He lives in the glen and probably has no intention of leaving it. He knows about farming and animals. What more do you want?'

*Love.* The word formed in her mind, but was never said because she thought he might laugh at her. Also she didn't really know yet what she meant by love. Occasionally she had thought during the past week or so that the dangerously lovely feeling of comradeship which she felt when she was with Duncan might be love. If it was, she thought ruefully, it looked as if she might be fated to love someone who didn't love her; someone who held himself aloof from her and who preferred red hair in a woman.

'Hello, you two. What are you doing here?'

The high, light voice belonged to Sandra. She was there beside the table, tall and striking in a stone-coloured suit with an emerald scarf which played up her white skin and satin-smooth red hair.

'We've been shopping,' replied Duncan, rising to his feet politely. 'And we've just finished eating.'

'What a pity I didn't know you wanted to come to Oban,' said Sandra, sweetly smiling at him and completely ignoring Jan. 'I could have brought you and saved Jan the trouble.'

'She came into town with me to help me blue my hard-earned pay,' he explained.

'Oh.' Sandra looked rather sulky and her eyes narrowed as she glanced at Jan. 'I'm here with Mother. We've been lunching with my aunt, Lady Carmichael. I'd have come across to talk to you earlier, but I couldn't very well leave them.'

So she had been there all the time sitting at a table in a secluded corner and probably watching them. Jan had a queer feeling that she had been spied upon and that all her expressions and gestures as she had talked and laughed with Duncan had been noted carefully and stored away in Sandra's mind to be used again later.

Duncan went to pay the bill, so she could do nothing else but accompany Sandra into the entrance hall which had lost its sunny somnolent silence and was full of people gathering together to go off on some outing.

As Duncan joined them again Sandra pushed a hand through his arm in rather a possessive gesture and said,

'I'd like you to come and meet my mother, Duncan. Over here.'

Mrs. Lang was saying good-bye to another slim, imperious-looking woman who was obviously her sister and when she turned back from the doorway she betrayed her surprise at seeing her daughter arm-in-arm with a casually dressed young man by raising her finely-plucked eyebrows. Then as she looked at Duncan more closely an expression of incredulity flashed across her face. It was gone almost as soon as it had appeared and when Sandra introduced Duncan with a touch of defiance in her manner, she nodded politely to him, then turned to Jan and smiled warmly.

'How nice to see you, Jan. How is your poor sister? Is she recovering?'

'Slowly. We're hoping she'll come home soon.'

'I'd like to see her when she comes. She's a very brave young woman. We'll be having open day at the castle soon. Why not bring her then, and stay for tea?' said Mrs. Lang. Then turning to Duncan she added, 'My daughter has told me you come from Australia and that your forebears may have emigrated there from the Highlands.'

'I believe that they might have done,' replied Duncan in his coolest and most polite manner.

'Have you any idea which area they came from?' queried Mrs. Lang, looking him up and down.

'No. But I'm hoping to find that out one day.'

'Then you should meet my husband,' said Mrs. Lang emphatically, much to Jan's surprise. 'He is an amateur genealogist and has a great interest in tracing the families of the descendants of people who emigrated from Scotland to other parts of the world. I'm sure he'll be able to help you.' She paused, stared closely at him again and then allowed herself a thinly-gracious smile. 'I would like very much for you to accompany Jan and her sister when they come over. Will you do that, Mr. Davidson?'

'I'll be very pleased to,' he said without hesitation.

'Now we must rush. So glad we bumped into you both,' said Mrs. Lang airily. 'Come along, Sandra. We have more shopping to do.'

With a triumphant smile at Duncan and a slightly patronizing one at Jan, Sandra dutifully followed her mother from the hotel.

It was odd how an unexpected meeting with two people and a few apparently innocuous remarks could change the mood of an outing. As she and Duncan drove back to the glen along the same road they had come that morning it seemed to Jan that everything looked pale and washed out even though the sun was shining with a warmer more mellow glow, its rays turning the sea into a pool of molten gold beyond which mountains were hidden in a haze of violet light.

The strong sense of comradeship with Duncan had gone. He had shut her out from his thoughts. Not that there was any law which insisted that he share every thought with her just because he was sharing the front seat of a vehicle with her, thought Jan ruefully, but she missed the feeling and had been unprepared for the strange desolation of spirit which had overcome her at the realization he had been pleased to see Sandra and even more pleased to receive an invitation to visit the castle.

'I hope you didn't accept the invitation to go to the castle just because you were invited to go with *me*,' she said, remembering how the evening before he had suspected she had offered to give him a lift into Oban today just because her mother had insisted that she should ask him.

He gave her an alert sidelong glance and then his grin drove an interesting and attractive crease down his cheek.

'No, mate, I didn't,' he replied. 'But I appreciate that I wouldn't have been invited if you hadn't been with me. Sandra isn't as dumb as she looks.'

'What do you mean?' she exclaimed. His remark about Sandra was hardly kind.

'If she hadn't seized the opportunity to introduce me to her mother while I was with you I wouldn't have been invited. You put the seal of respectability on me.'

So that was why Sandra had looked triumphant and why Duncan himself looked so pleased with life. They had made a great stride forward in their relationship. He had been invited to Sandra's home by no less a personage then her snobbish mother, and Jan Reid had been the pawn they had used to achieve that aim.

Jan suddenly found that her thoughts were chaotic and that she was blinking back the tears as she realized that the outing with her had meant no more to Duncan than any other pay-day spree and she meant no more to him than any other girl. The enchantment had been only for her, not for him.

'When do you expect your sister back from hospital?' he asked, and the question showed that he was still thinking about the invitation and wanted to know how soon he might be going to the castle.

'Mother says that she should be home about the end of the month. Gordie and Chris may go down and bring her back by car. Of course she may not want to come back to the glen, so don't count on her being here to be invited to tea at the castle,' she said rather tartly.

'I won't,' he answered smoothly. 'But you're still invited and I shall come with you.'

'Supposing I refuse?' she flared independently. 'What will you do then?'

'I shall just have to find another way of being invited,' he said lightly. They were on the last stretch of road before the ferry and he changed down the gears to take the steep descent to the pier.

'You're very keen to go,' she sniped.

'Wouldn't you be if there was a chance of meeting a well-known amateur genealogist who might be able to help you trace your forebears?' There was a touch of irony in his voice now which brought her glance round to him again. He was looking straight ahead with narrowed eyes, and the determined set to his firm chiselled mouth struck her as being ruthless.

'That isn't your only reason for wanting to go to the castle to meet the Colonel,' she accused, and he gave her an alert glance out of the corners of his eyes.

'You're right, it isn't,' he drawled coolly. 'Don't forget, I have a liking for red hair.'

It hurt. It pushed her away as he intended it should and the drive to the ferry continued in silence, not the pleasant easy silence of comradeship but a tense silence during which Jan was very aware of every move Duncan made and almost every breath he took.

Golden light dappled the smooth water of the loch as the ferry sidled crabwise across the incoming tide. It also caressed the brown moors and soaring grey ridges of Ben Dearg, softening harsh contours into sweeping smooth curves, rising to the sharp dazzling peak.

The ferry bumped into the landing pier, the crewman

drew back the gate and the Land-Rover trundled on to land again. Along the road they sped beside the tumbling flashing river past clumps of Scots pine, under drooping birches. Before them as they climbed up the glen slowly the moorland opened out, brown and green, scattered with outcrops of rock and spotted with sheep. Past the end of the lane to Tighnacoarach they sped and Jan had a quick glimpse of her father walking across a field, his crook in his hand, the two sheepdogs at his heels.

Up the rutted unmade part of the road they went and swerved left through a broken dyke on to a narrow over-grown path, towards the long low cottage which looked down over the field and moorland to the distant loch with the village glinting along its shore and the squat grey tower of the castle on the other shore peeping from amongst the trees which surrounded it.

As she got down from the vehicle Jan noticed differences in the cottage. Glass was in the windows which had once been open to the weather. A new door had been fitted on the byre. The tangle of grass and weeds which had choked the small garden had been cleared away and the few small shrubs which grew there were thrusting forth new leaves as if delighted to see the sun-light once more. Duncan had been very busy in his spare time.

He had backed the vehicle up to the door of the byre and Jan helped him to carry the lengths of timber into the low-roofed building to store them there. When that was done they both went back to the Land-Rover and he waited for her to climb into the driver's seat. This time he offered no invitation to her to enter the house and share a tinker's brew with him.

The ending was so different from the beginning. Being young and optimistic she had set forth that morning in expectation which had been far greater than realization. Now her disappointment showed, although she did not know that it did, in the droop of her mouth, in the slump of her shoulders and in her uncharacteristic silence.

With his hand on the door of the vehicle ready to slam it shut, Duncan glanced at her. Then he leaned forward and said gently,

'Thanks for the help, Jan. You're a great sport and we had a good pay-day together.'

Surprised by this statement, she looked at him. He bent his head and kissed her on the mouth. His lips were cool and firm against hers and their unexpected pressure drew forth a spontaneous response from her. He withdrew quickly, slammed the door and strode off into the cottage without a backward glance.

Although his kiss had been gentle her mouth seemed to burn as she guided the lurching vehicle along the path and down the road. She was bewildered, not so much by his gesture but by her own response to it, and she had an uneasy feeling that the day, pleasant though it had been, marked an end to one remarkably uncomplicated phase of her life and the beginning of another which would prove complicated and possibly painful.

# CHAPTER FOUR

The voices of the choir gathered together in a crescendo of sound as a wave of the sea gathers itself before its long-diminishing plunge towards land. A long note was held, then, with a sudden shift of key and twist of rhythm, the voices fell away to a sighing whisper like the sound of the sea washing the walls of the great rocky caverns of the islands as a lonely solo soprano brought to an end the Hebridean lament known as *Sea-Sorrow*.

After the sound had died away there was a moment of silent tranquillity in the hall. Then Molly Robertson spoke quietly as if afraid to disturb the peaceful atmosphere produced by the haunting melody. When she had finished the choir broke up into its usual chattering groups and inevitably Jan found herself talking to Colin, an occurrence which had happened often lately.

For with the end of the lambing season she had been able to return to the choir practices. At the first one she had attended after the outing with Duncan to Oban she had had difficulty in ignoring the sudden wild beating of her heart and the rush of colour to her face when Duncan had entered the hall. Her reaction had alarmed her and on returning home she had given herself a good talking to, warning herself about the dangers of infatuation. Her inherent native caution had taken over as she had reminded herself that Duncan himself had told her that he was more interested in Sandra than he was in her.

So, with common sense subduing her natural instinct to be attracted by someone who was different from herself in so many ways yet with whom she had on several occasions experienced a brief and exciting unity of spirit, she turned her mind away from him determinedly.

In turning away she had applied herself enthusiastically to her work about the farm, taking pleasure in the changes brought about in the glen as the month of May advanced. New grass, vivid and succulent, sprang up across field and moor. Patches of dormant heather came to life and took on a warmer purplish-brown in preparation for the blaze of colour which would come later in the summer. The bare black winter silhouettes of deciduous trees disappeared under a fluttering froth of new leaves and dainty pink, white and yellow petals, blown from blossom, wafted about on the sea breeze and collected in drifts in corners which had so recently held snow.

Everywhere there was the sound of lambs bleating as the tiny bundles of white wool leapt high in the air in sheer delight of living. Then their cries would be drowned by the noise of a busy tractor moving across a field with seagulls and crows in its wake as the plough shares turned over the dark soil.

In keeping her mind turned away from the owner of Tigh Uisdean Jan had become more involved with Colin. After choir he usually walked with her and her mother to the hotel to have a drink and join in the general family and village gossip with Chris and Gordon. Several times he had invited her to go for an afternoon sail with him at the week-ends in his small racing sloop which was now moored with several other boats in a sheltered corner of the loch near the old jetty.

Now with the chatter of the choir members going on around them Jan was describing an incident at the farm which had happened that morning, aware that Colin was only half-listening as he watched, with narrowed eyes and frowning brows, Sandra approaching Duncan, touching him on the arm to get his attention and then smiling up at the tall Australian.

'I'm still bothered by his likeness to that portrait I saw somewhere,' muttered Colin, frowning even more as Duncan gallantly held Sandra's coat for her while she slipped her arms into its sleeves.

'Have you remembered where you saw the portrait yet?' asked Jan.

'No, I haven't. It was some years ago and it was in a dark dusty place where you wouldn't normally see a painting like that. It wasn't on the wall of a house and it wasn't in an art gallery or exhibition of any sort. It could have been in Edinburgh or some other part of the country for all I know,' he replied with a touch of irritation. 'I wish I could remember. It might be useful to know.'

'I told Duncan about it once,' said Jan. 'He said I must tell him when you remember. He'd like to see it. You see, he's trying to trace his ancestors. He thinks they must have lived in the Highlands.'

'Davidson,' murmured Colin. 'It's a common enough name, but he might have a bit of trouble if he doesn't know which region of the country they lived in.'

'I've been thinking that it's not his real name,' said Jan quietly, watching Sandra and Duncan leaving the hall together.

'What makes you think that?' asked Colin sharply.

'Just a feeling I have. You could call it intuition if you like.'

'Don't tell me you're becoming psychic like your grandmother? They say it runs in families, you know,' he said derisively, although interest was there sparkling in his shrewd eyes.

'No, I don't think I am. I'm going by a conversation I had with Duncan when he first came here. I had to ask him for his second name and he told me quite frankly that he had adopted the name Duncan.'

'Did he now?' murmured Colin. 'How very interesting. So you're thinking he's hiding his real identity, do you?' He considered this for a moment then shook his head. 'Ach, no, I don't see how he could. He'd have to have documents – a passport. Have you forgotten he's an immigrant?'

'I suppose you're right,' admitted Jan with a sigh. 'But do you think Andrew Forbes would ask to see his passport?'

Colin gave his suggestion some thought and came to a conclusion based on his knowledge of Andrew.

'No, I don't think he would. He'd be so glad to get someone to take Tigh Uisdean over that I think he'd accept Duncan on face value,' he said.

'Sandra says she feels she's met Duncan somewhere before. She even said so to him, but he denied it.'

'She could have been using it as a conversational gambit,' said Colin dryly. 'A way of getting to know him better. I see they've left together again. I wonder where they'll park to do their lovemaking tonight?'

'Ach, what a thing to say!' exclaimed Jan, slightly shocked.

Colin was not at all repentant.

'Surely you're not thinking that their association is entirely platonic?' he jeered. 'If ever there was a case of physical attraction, that's it. Hey, where are you going?'

'I don't like that kind of remark,' retorted Jan with mock primness in an attempt to hide the fact that the thought of Duncan making love to Sandra surreptitiously in a parked car had upset her. She had not thought that Duncan would behave like that. 'Also I don't want Mother to go to Chris's without me,' she added.

'You may not like it, but I was only being realistic,' replied Colin seriously, holding the hall door open for her to go through. 'I'm not one for burying my head in the sand and I know Sandra pretty well. Anyway, you've surely been hearing the gossip about them?'

'What gossip?'

'Sandra's car has been seen several times parked off the road in secluded places late at night and it's also been seen coming down from the head of the glen. Naturally those who have seen her here with Duncan have drawn their own conclusions.'

'Not very nice ones,' said Jan rather stiffly.

'That's true, but possibly correct ones, Sandra being the sort of person she is.' Again Colin's voice was dry and she looked at him sharply. He looked rather grim. Then with an effort to throw off his grimness he said, 'Let's forget them and think about us. Would you like to come to a dance organized by the yacht club? It's being held in Oban.'

Surprised by the invitation, Jan turned to face him squarely under the light over the doorway. In his well-scrubbed, well-barbered way he was good-looking. His sun-bleached brown hair waved crisply and his weather-beaten, rather cherubic face glowed with good health. She knew from her recent outings with him that his outlook on life was similar to her own. He loved being out of doors. He liked animals. He believed there was no better place to live than the glen. He was eligible, there was no doubt of that. Was it possible, as Duncan had suggested, that Colin had been waiting for her to grow up and that his casual invitations to go sailing with him or dancing with him were the preliminaries to courtship?

There was only one way to find out, and that was to go to the dance with him; to go sailing with him this summer and see what evolved.

'I'd like to go,' she replied simply.

'Ach, that's fine. I'll be seeing you again before then and we can make arrangements.'

Now there was the problem of what she should wear for such a dance, and she took that problem to her mother and Chris that same evening.

'You'll be needing a long one for that affair,' said Chris. 'You could be making one. There's time.'

'Aye, and you could be finding the material in Glasgow. Chris is going down to fetch Ellen home. You could go with her,' said Sheena. 'The ward Sister says she's going to be released next Friday, but she doesn't want to travel by public transport. I'm thinking she'll be a wee bit self-conscious of the marks on her face. You could leave here on the Wednesday, having all Thursday for shopping, and come back Friday.'

'Aye, that's a good idea,' agreed Chris. 'It's time we three got together for a wee while.'

Pleased at the idea of going shopping in Glasgow, Jan worked blithely all day. It was a sunny, blustery day full of birds cries. Returning from the hill after counting the sheep she came across her mother and Duncan just leaving one of the barns together.

'I've been showing Duncan those old chairs that I have stored in there. He may as well be using them. They're only collecting dust,' explained Sheena. 'Will you not come in for a cup of tea, Duncan? My mother-in-law is forever complaining that she hasn't met you yet.'

As Jan guessed he would, he hesitated. His bright blue gaze came round to her, saw the challenge in her dark eyes. A faintly mocking smile curved his mouth.

'I can see that if I refuse I shall be considered a coward by Little Bo-Peep,' he murmured, and Jan could have laughed aloud at the mystification expressed on her mother's face.

'I don't know about Bo-Peep's opinion of you, but I do know we'll all be thinking we're not good enough for you if you go on refusing to come in,' retorted Sheena tartly. 'However, you can please yourself.'

She turned with a toss of her head and went into the house. Duncan gazed after her rather regretfully.

'Now I've offended her after she's been good enough to look out some furniture for me. What shall I do to make amends?' he said.

'Come in and have tea,' replied Jan, 'and all will be forgiven.'

He followed her into the house and she introduced him to Agnes immediately. Her grandmother's thin claw-like hand reached up and was engulfed in Duncan's big, yet graceful, capable hand.

'Ach, 'tis a bonny lad you are,' said Agnes in her soft singing voice. 'I'm thinking that Davey would grow up to look like you, tall and straight. You only grow like that if you've lived in a place where the sun is bright and strong so that you walk with your head held high trying to reach up to it. They tell me the sun shines like that in Australia and that you've come from there.'

She tilted her head to one side and her faded eyes looked up and over his head. Jan felt a little niggle of uneasiness as she recognized the sign of the second sight.

'You've brought a message for me from Davey?' asked Agnes, and Jan shivered a little.

There was a curious little silence. Duncan's glance shifted first to Sheena's face and then to Jan's. He had gone pale and Jan had the strangest feeling that he knew what her grandmother was talking about but was unwilling to admit that he did.

'Now, Mother, what are you going on about?' said Sheena in her sharp matter-of-fact way.

'I'm talking about Davey who used to live at Tigh Uisdean. Remember I was after telling you that he said he was going to Australia with his father and that one day they would have a sheep farm which would be bigger than this one,' sighed Agnes.

'Australia is a big place, ma'am,' said Duncan gently, 'and the chances of me ever having met your friend are very remote. Forgive me for saying so, but if he's alive he must be a great age.'

'Aye, I was forgetting that,' sighed Agnes, her eyes focussing properly on his face. 'My memory isn't as good as it was and it plays tricks on me. Fifteen he was when he went away, and I was ten. His hair was black as jet and his eyes were as blue as periwinkles. You remind me of him, so you do. What did you say your last name was? Davidson? David's son. Aye, I was thinking that maybe you were his son came back to the house of your father, but I can see now that you're too young for that. Away with you now to the table and be having your tea, lad.'

By now Duncan's face was quite white, but he made no comment as he turned to the table as he had been bidden to take his tea. Although his normal colour gradually returned he seemed abstracted as her father talked to him about farm matters, and several times Jan noticed that he glanced warily at her grandmother.

When Duncan stood up to take his leave Jan made an excuse to go out with him, saying that she hadn't finished counting the sheep. He gave her a surprised glance but did not dissuade her, and together they walked across the windy farmyard, through the gate and out on to the sunlit hillside.

'I hear that you're off to the city tomorrow to fetch your sister,' he said, breaking the silence first.

Ahead of them in the clear afternoon sunlight the mountain looked very near. Already the lower slopes were a lush green as bracken fronds unfurled themselves and higher up the runnelled grey-green rock seemed to shimmer with golden light.

'Yes, I am,' said Jan, rather absently, then taking a deep breath she plunged into a subject which had been bothering her ever since the choir practice of the previous night. 'Duncan, I think I'd best be warning you that people are beginning to talk about you and Sandra.'

She had done it, and now she was holding herself tense awaiting his reaction, unable to predict how he would answer.

'What are they saying?' he asked at last, rather indifferently, she thought, as if he didn't care what people said about him.

Being stepped in so far she had to go on, even though she had only Colin's word that there was gossip going about.

'You've been seen several times in her car.'

It was extraordinarily difficult to say any more than that without feeling embarrassed.

'So?' He drawled the word and ice edged the usual warmth of his voice. 'Is it forbidden for the laird's daughter to give a mere crofter a lift occasionally?'

'No, only . . .' His sidelong glance was a flash of frosty blue and she was quite unable to continue.

'Only what?' he prompted softly.

She was trapped. Why had she ever thought she could warn him about the gossip? Why had she ever thought he should be warned? He was not as easy to approach as she had hoped.

Looking away over the hillside to the dry-stone dykes, she noticed for the first time that a new gate had been hung in the gap known as Bealach Glas. The way on to the croft of Tigh Uisdean was barred.

'Ach, you've put a gate in the dyke,' she exclaimed rather foolishly.

'Of course I have. Now that the field beyond it is ploughed and set with potatoes I don't want any sheep straying on to it,' he replied coolly, and she had the oddest feeling that he lumped her with the stray sheep. 'But that isn't what you were going to say. Come on, Bo-Peep, let's have it. What's on your mind?'

He sounded irritable, impatient with her, and she missed the friendliness which had underscored all their other meetings. The deep gulf of differences yawned between them: differences in age, in upbringing, in experiences, in temperament, and she wondered how she could ever have known those brief moments of unity with him. Perhaps they had never been. Perhaps they had been only in her imagination.

'Don't tell me you've forgotten what you were going to say,' he jeered quietly, and she gave him a wary sideways glance. They had reached the new white gate and he was leaning against it, looking down into the glen, his eyes slitted against the bright glare of the westering sun.

'No, I haven't,' she retorted, needled by his manner. 'It's just that it's so difficult to tell you. It's not the lifts exactly that people are gossiping about. Sandra's car has been seen parked off the road late at night, in secluded places, and naturally since you've been seen with her, nasty conclusions are being drawn.'

Now that it was out she looked appealingly at him. His narrowed gaze shifted from the distant view to her face. His eyes were as blue and cold as the loch on a frosty day.

'Do *you* believe what they're saying?' he asked.

Did he really care what she believed? She had a sudden longing to cast caution aside and cry out that she believed only in him, but that innate native caution refused to be cast aside easily.

'I don't want to,' she mumbled, avoiding his eyes.

'I suppose I should be grateful for that small show of support,' he remarked sardonically. 'I'm going to reward you by telling you that contrary to local speculation I have not been with Sandra when her car has been seen parked off the road late at night in a secluded spot.'

'She's also been seen coming down the glen road late at night, and I know she hasn't been visiting us,' Jan mumbled miserably.

'Is this standard treatment of newcomers to your glen?' he queried, still sardonic. 'A smear campaign? Let's make life uncomfortable for him so that he'll move on? It sounds very much to me as if someone is objecting to my presence here, and even more to my friendship with Sandra.'

Jan stared at him in abject silence, thinking of the person who was her source of information, Colin. Would he deliberately manufacture gossip which blackened Duncan's reputation? And if so, why?

'I'm sorry, Duncan,' she whispered. 'I was only trying to warn you.'

'About doing something which I haven't done,' he said

with a rather wry smile. 'O.K., mate, thanks for the tip. Are you going to ask Sandra whom she's meeting on the sly?'

'Ach, no, I couldn't,' she protested hotly.

'Then all I can say is it looks as if you've stumbled on another mystery. It's been quite an informative afternoon one way and another. Your grandmother really rattled me. You see, that old sheep-shearer I used to know, the one who had come from the Highlands, his name was Davey, but I never knew his last name.'

Relieved because he had changed the subject and because the ice had gone from his voice, Jan answered eagerly.

'You said that you used to think he could have been your grandfather. What did you mean?' she asked.

'Just that. He could have been my grandfather in that he was old enough to have been, but I didn't know in actual fact whether he was.' He gave her a quick glance, came to a decision and announced abruptly, 'I don't know who my father was, either.'

The mystery of Duncan was explained at last. Everything seemed suddenly brighter.

'So you're an orphan,' she exclaimed, smiling up at him. 'I'm glad!'

He stared at her in surprise and then began to laugh.

'Well, if you aren't the strangest girl I've ever met! Why are you glad because you think I'm an orphan? I've always been led to believe that being an orphan is a sad state of affairs and that one should always feel sorry for such a person.'

Meeting his derisive glance, she felt confused and had the oddest feeling that she had betrayed her feelings concerning him.

'I meant I'm glad you're an orphan because that explains your adoption of the name Duncan,' she muttered.

'Does it?' he queried. 'I fail to see how myself, but if it satisfies that little maggot of curiosity which wriggles around inside you and gives you no peace until you've found an answer of some sort, I'll go along with the idea.'

He lunged away from the gate, opened it and stepped through, closing it after him. Leaning his arms on the top bar, he grinned down at her. 'Here we are standing in that magic place again, so I think it's safer for us both if the gate is between us. Have a good trip to Glasgow. I'll be seeing you.'

He turned away and began to walk round the edge of the ploughed field. Puzzled by his parting remark about the magic place, Jan sighed and made her way back home.

At least she knew a little more about Duncan. Or did she? All he had told her was the fact that he did not know who his father was. She had leapt to the conclusion that he was an orphan. Once again he had baffled her by seeming to give her information about himself, and when she scrutinized that information she discovered she had learned precisely nothing.

During the next two days, however, Jan had little time to spare to puzzle over the mystery of Duncan. The drive down to Glasgow through the Pass of Brander, along Glen Lochy to Crianlarich, beside Loch Lomond, down to Dumbarton where they stayed the night with their Aunt Helen, Sheena's sister, was made without mishap in spite of the perpetual drizzling rain which hid the heads of the mountains and made the moors look a uniform sodden grey.

After a good night's rest they went on to Glasgow, shopped in Sauchiehall Street and then made their way to the hospital to see Ellen.

She was a different Ellen, with a thin drawn face still bearing the shiny scars of skin grafting on her right cheek. Her big expressive eyes seemed darker and bigger than ever and her beautiful hands were still covered with bandages.

When she saw them she broke down and wept. Discarding their normal native dislike of showing emotion in public, Chris and Jan wept, too, on seeing the marks on Ellen's lovely face. But soon they were all laughing through their tears at some joke which Chris made, and because they were glad to be together.

After making arrangements to collect Ellen the next morning they went to Bearsden to stay the night with an old school friend of Chris's, leaving there early in the morning to drive back to the hospital. It was almost eleven before they eventually left the city and drove westward to Dumbarton to have lunch with their aunt. Then as sunlight broke through the clouds which had hovered all morning they set off north for home.

It was a happy journey. Chris drove as far as Crianlarich where they stopped for tea in the hotel. From there Jan took over the driving, singing softly to herself as the road wound westward over wide stretches of sunlit moorland and beside glittering lochs.

By the time they reached Glen Dearg it was almost dark, and it was there that the first argument of the day broke out between Chris and Ellen. Chris wanted them all to go to the hotel and have their supper there, but Ellen shrank from having to meet anyone outside the family so soon and said she wanted to go straight home. In the end Jan took sides with Ellen and turned right as they left the ferry and took the road through the glen.

Half-way to Tighnacoarach she had to pull over sharply to the left side of the road to allow a car which was coming down to pass. It flashed by at great speed.

'Who was that?' asked Ellen, who knew that not many cars took that road unless they were going to the farm.

'Looked like Sandra's car to me,' said Chris.

'You mean Sandra Lang?' asked Ellen. 'What would she be doing on this road at night? Surely she hasn't been visiting Mother and Dad?'

'I doubt it,' said Chris dryly. 'She's probably been taking her supper at Tigh Uisdean. She's been spending a lot of her time up there recently from all accounts.'

'But it's empty,' exclaimed Ellen.

'Not now it isn't,' replied Chris. 'There've been some changes since you were last home. Not only has Sandra come back to live at the castle but we also have a handsome stranger living at Tigh Uisdean. He's an Australian and no one can quite get the measure of him. But one thing is certain, he's making a conquest where the local heiress is concerned. I daresay Jan can tell you more than I can. She sees more of them than I do at the choir practices.'

'Sandra in the choir?' squeaked Ellen. 'I can't imagine that. She was always far too snooty to join in village activities.'

'Ach, well, pride has a way of taking a fall now and again,' murmured Chris. 'And Sandra's must have been in the dust for a while after her engagement was broken off.'

'It's such an age since anyone new came to the glen or anything happened here that I feel quite annoyed that something has happened while I've been away,' muttered Ellen.

'Things have been happening all right. The stranger has given us plenty to gossip about.' Again Chris's voice had a sardonic crispness and Jan had difficulty in not rushing to Duncan's defence. To do so would have drawn Ellen's attention to her and she knew from past experience how her sister could torment and tease. As she guided the car along the lane to the farmhouse she half-listened to Chris telling Ellen all she knew about Duncan.

'I can hardly wait to meet him,' said Ellen eventually. 'He must be someone very special if he has Mother supplying him with bits of furniture and Dad giving him

115

work to do and lending him farm equipment as well as having Sandra driving up and down the glen road to visit him. Whatever will he do next?'

'Marry Sandra, is my guess, and I'm not the only one in the glen thinking along those lines. He'll probably have to, the way she's throwing herself at him,' said Chris. 'What do you think, Jan?'

Jan didn't answer. She could not trust herself to speak. She was thinking that although Duncan had denied that he had been with Sandra in her car when it had been seen parked off the road he had not denied that Sandra had visited him at Tigh Uisdean.

She parked the car and switched off the engine, hoping that her sisters had not noticed her lack of response, but she might have known that the quick-witted Ellen would notice.

'You're remarkably quiet on the subject of the stranger,' Ellen said, about to follow Chris out of the car. 'No opinion to give on him?'

'No, not really,' mumbled Jan as she opened the door.

'Don't you like him?' probed Ellen shrewdly.

'Not much.' She got out of the car quickly, slammed the door and went straight into the house before Ellen could ask any more questions.

During the next few days while Ellen adjusted to being at home and struggled to overcome her reluctance to meet the relatives and friends who called to see her and wish her well, she showed no urge to torment her youngest sister. At first her mood was brittle and defensive as she braved the surreptitious glances which were directed at the scars on her face and at her very short hair, but as she began to respond to her mother's fond cosseting and her father's quiet but ungrudging admiration, she relaxed and actually seemed to be happy to stay at home. The actress in her came to life again as she told the story of the fire over and over again to those who asked her about it, and after a while it was noticeable that the actual telling of the tale was having a therapeutic effect on her.

One of her visitors was Sandra who reissued the invitation for Jan and Ellen to have tea at the castle.

'We thought you could come on the day that the old part of the castle and the gardens are open to the public for the first time this year. Mother has arranged for tea to be served in the old banqueting hall, which has been restored. You won't forget to bring Duncan, will you, Jan?' she said.

'I'm not sure whether I want to go,' muttered Ellen, her hand going to her cheek, her eyes suddenly dark with unspoken anxiety at the thought of braving a crowd.

'You needn't think everyone will be looking at you,' scoffed Sandra rather callously. 'You know, Ellen, if you're going to let a little mark like that make you self-conscious for the rest of your life you're not going to have much fun, are you?'

The heartless remarks seemed to have a beneficial effect on Ellen. She stiffened slightly and her eyes flashed angrily, then narrowed as her brilliant smile appeared.

'No, I'm not, am I?' she murmured. 'Very well, I shall come. Of course I can't speak for Jan.'

'I'll go if you're going,' said Jan.

'And bring Duncan?' queried Sandra.

'Only if he wants to go.'

'Oh, he wants to go,' said Sandra with smug confidence. 'But it will look better if he comes with you. After all, Mother did invite him to come with you. It's the only way she'll accept him for the time being. I'm hoping all that will change when Daddy meets him. I hope you don't mind helping him in this way, Jan?'

Sandra turned on the charm, smiling at Jan in a conspiratorial way as if they shared a secret.

'I don't seem to have much choice, do I?' sighed Jan with a wry grin.

When Sandra had gone Ellen questioned Jan about the

heiress's relationship with Duncan and Jan told her all that she knew.

'So it's a case of jilted heiress on the rebound falls for stranger,' remarked Ellen. 'Have you any idea why the Honourable James jilted Sandra?'

'She told me it was a mutual agreement. They decided that they were incompatible, but Mrs. Lang had a different tale. She said that James dropped Sandra because she wouldn't lower the standard of behaviour to the level of that of the young women he was used to going about with.'

Ellen's eyes opened wide.

'Oh, I see. She wouldn't anticipate marriage?' she said, and when Jan nodded in agreement, she added, 'Doesn't sound like the Sandra I used to know. I wouldn't be surprised if it was the other way round and that the Honourable James was the one who wouldn't lower his standards to those of Sandra. She was always inclined to throw herself at any eligible man in her vicinity. Even Andrew once said—' She broke off abruptly and her face closed up. When she spoke again her voice was deliberately light. 'Shall we do the hem on your dress now? Put it on and I'll pin it in place.'

The subject of Sandra and her possible designs on Andrew Forbes at one time was shelved neatly and apparently forgotten by Ellen. But Jan was not deceived. Of all the people in the glen who knew Ellen, Andrew was the only one who had not come to see her during the past two weeks, and she guessed that his non-appearance hurt her sister. There wasn't even a message from him by way of Chris, although the latter asked Ellen to go down to the hotel for the evening several times and Jan wondered whether she did so in the hopes of bringing Ellen and Andrew face to face. But Ellen was still refusing to go out into a public place and unless Andrew came to the farm there didn't seem to be any chance of them meeting in the near future.

On the last night of May, Jan duly went off to Oban with Colin to the yacht club dance. It was a merry affair and she forgot the problem of Ellen and Andrew and the mystery of Duncan as she participated in every dance from the graceful and complicated strathspeys and reels of her own country to more modern but no less energetic dances. Colonel and Mrs. Lang were there as he was one of the flag-officers of the club, but there was no sign of Sandra.

Returning home in the small hours of the morning almost asleep as she sat beside Colin, Jan was startled when he had to pull the car over to the left side of the glen road as a fast-moving car without headlights sped past them.

After a few choice unpleasant words about idiot drivers who lacked consideration for others who used the road, Colin added disgustedly,

'I suppose that was Sandra. She's taking a chance staying up at the croft until this hour. I wonder what sort of excuse she gives to her parents for staying out half the night? Looks as if gossip hasn't been telling lies.'

Jan said nothing. She was thinking that now she had seen a car that could be Sandra's coming twice from the direction of Tigh Uisdean she could only believe that the gossip was very near to the truth.

'Well, here you are home again, safe and sound,' said Colin with a forced heartiness as he drove into the farm-yard, stopped the estate car and doused the lights. 'Did you enjoy the dance?'

'Yes, I did. Thanks for taking me,' she replied, picking up her evening bag and wrapping the gossamer-light Shetland shawl which her mother had lent her for the evening around her.

'Is that all the thanks I get?' challenged Colin, and she half-turned back in surprise. He put an arm round her shoulders and bent towards her. As his mouth touched hers Jan didn't resist. After all, she had to find out somehow if Duncan was right and Colin was really eligible. She tried not to think of that other first kiss, but inevitably she made comparisons. Noticing her lack of response, Colin withdrew and said rather irritably,

'It's high time you were growing up, Jan Reid. Is that the best you can do when someone kisses you good night?'

In the darkness her cheeks flamed and she felt a strong urge to slap him.

'Ach, just because I'm not like some other lasses you've taken to dances, Colin Matheson, there's no reason for you to make a remark like that,' she retorted. 'I don't go around kissing all and sundry.'

'That's obvious,' he jibed nastily. 'But I wouldn't mind betting that you'd react differently if your crofter friend kissed you.'

'I wish you'd stop referring to him as my crofter friend!' she flared, her face hot again as she recalled how she had wished Duncan's kiss could have gone on longer and led to more. 'He isn't any more friendly with me than with anyone else. Have you forgotten that it's Sandra he's friendly with?'

'No, I haven't,' he muttered, and it sounded as if he was speaking between clenched teeth. 'And I can't help wishing he hadn't come to live in the glen. We can do without his sort.'

This remark surprised her. It sounded so unlike the cheerful happy-go-lucky person she knew Colin to be.

'Why do you dislike him?' she asked.

'I have my reasons,' he growled darkly, then added rather sheepishly, 'I'm sorry I said what I did, Jan. We had a good time tonight. I'll see you at choir practice on Monday.'

But on Monday evening he wasn't at choir practice, and neither was Duncan. In fact no one in the family or the village had seen Duncan during the last few days, a circumstance which seemed to worry Sandra, who came over to speak to Jan when the practice was finished.

'Do you think he's left the glen?' she asked.

'I'm sorry I can't help you,' replied Jan stiffly. 'I'm not one for going up to the croft all the time, even though he lives next door.'

Sandra's eyes sparkled with malice as the remark found its target.

'I didn't suppose you were,' she said coldly. 'The veterinary surgeon is much more to your taste, I'm sure. After all, you have so much in common – an interest in animals and farming. I can imagine you both making an excellent if rather dull married couple discussing the amount of milk produced by Rosie the prize Jersey cow and the amount of wool the flock of sheep will provide the next time they're clipped.'

She turned on her heel and left the hall. Jan blinked after her, bewildered by the sudden attack. She had not thought Sandra paid so much attention to other people's affairs.

The week took its course without any sign of Duncan, and on Friday Jan began to wonder whether he intended to go with her and Ellen to the castle the next day when it would be open to the public for the first time.

'You'd better go up to the croft and see if he's there,' suggested Ellen practically, and added a shade too casually, 'Have you seen anything of Andrew lately?'

'Not for weeks. He was here one day after you were burned. I told him about the accident,' replied Jan eagerly, glad that at last Ellen had brought up the subject which was obviously worrying her most.

'What did he say?'

'That he was sorry you'd been hurt. Why did you refuse to marry him when he asked you at New Year?'

Ellen turned away to look out of the kitchen window.

'Oh, because we're always arguing. Imagine going through life always disagreeing with the man you've married. He's so old-fashioned,' she replied vaguely.

'In what ways?'

'He thinks a woman should give up her career once she's married and always live in the same place as her husband, and I can't agree with him, that's all.'

Jan, who was ironing clothes, finished pressing a blouse before she answered, thinking about the situation seriously.

'But surely if you really love one another you should be willing to compromise and come to some arrangement which would suit you both,' she murmured eventually.

Ellen gave her a surprised yet slightly mocking glance.

'Hark to the wise shepherdess,' she remarked. 'How do you know so much? Are you in love?'

The question confused Jan and she couldn't answer, so Ellen turned away to look out of the window again, her attention caught by a movement in the farmyard.

'There he is, I think,' she exclaimed suddenly. 'The man from Tigh Uisdean. Quick, Jan, go and ask him in for a cup of tea and we can make arrangements with him about tomorrow.'

'He may not come,' replied Jan weakly, trying to hide the leap of delight she felt at the knowledge that Duncan was still at the croft, yet not wanting to go out and speak to him at such short notice.

'Why not? He must have come in before,' said Ellen.

'Gran makes him feel uncomfortable,' argued Jan.

'But Gran isn't here today. Go on, Jan, ask him,' urged Ellen, then turning, she caught sight of Jan's scarlet cheeks. 'Why, I do believe you want to keep him to yourself,' she taunted. 'You don't want me to meet him.'

'That's not true!' flared Jan, and Ellen smiled knowingly.

'I thought as much. The stranger hasn't only made a big impression on Sandra, he's also captivated my youngest sister, so I think it's high time I met him. I'll go and invite him to come in myself.'

She marched out through the back door into the sunshine and Jan, her heart still thudding and her cheeks burning, filled the kettle and plugged it in. She had just turned back to the ironing board when the sound of running feet startled her. The back door banged and Ellen appeared suddenly in the kitchen. She closed the inner door and leaned against it for a moment. Her face was chalk white.

'What's the matter?' exclaimed Jan.

'Nothing,' replied Ellen, and running across the room she disappeared through the door leading to the hall. Jan heard her footsteps on the stairs and then the far-off bang of a bedroom door being closed violently.

Bewildered by her sister's strange behaviour, Jan turned as the door from the porch opened, fully expecting to see Duncan enter. But instead of him her father strode in, followed by Andrew Forbes.

'Sit you down, Andrew,' said John Reid. 'Where's Ellen, Jan?'

'She's upstairs, lying down, having a rest,' stuttered Jan. 'She's not feeling herself this afternoon.'

If Andrew was disappointed by Ellen's absence he did not show it. He merely nodded and said,

'I understand.' He gave Jan a searching underbrowed glance, then asked abruptly, 'Have you seen anyone strange loitering about the moors lately?'

'No. Why do you ask?'

'I've been thinking for some time that someone is poaching the river and that they might one day take a fancy to some of the game in the forest. Today I came across something which made me sure.'

Jan felt herself going cold inside. By game she knew Andrew meant the red deer which roamed about the Dunmore forest. This time of the year was a close season for the hinds laid down by law, and anyone caught hunting them could be punished. In any case, only people invited to do so by the Colonel could hunt the deer during the hunting season in order to keep the numbers down so that the animals would not destroy the forest.

'What did you find?' she asked.

'A hind, dead of a gunshot wound. It must have been shot in the dark and it escaped. Someone is poaching at night – the old trick, I suppose, using a strong flashlight to mesmerize the animal and then shooting it carelessly and leaving it to die.'

'How cruel,' said Jan with a little shudder. 'I haven't seen any stranger in the glen.'

'What about Davidson? Do you think he would poach?'

'Ach, just because he's living in Hugh MacClachan's house there's no need to be thinking he's like Hugh,' replied Jan defensively.

Amusement flickered briefly in Andrew's grey eyes.

'Since I was born long after Hugh MacClachan left the glen I can hardly be likening Davidson to him,' he said. 'What do you think, John? You've had the lad working here. You should have his measure by now.'

Jan held her breath while her father took a few reflective puffs at his pipe.

'He's a good enough worker, I'm thinking,' he said at last. 'But he's still a mystery. He's not what he makes out to be. But I wouldn't be branding him a poacher until he's caught redhanded.'

Andrew nodded.

'Aye, I see what you mean,' he said. 'A man is innocent until he's proven guilty. Well, I'll be leaving it at that for a while, but I hope you'll be keeping your eyes skinned for anything unusual. I hear you're expected at the castle on Saturday, Jan.'

'Ellen too,' she said.

Again he nodded and began to talk farming news to her father while she made the tea.

Perturbed by Andrew's suggestion that poachers might

have been approaching the estate across either the farm land or by way of Duncan's croft, as well as by his suspicions of Duncan, Jan decided that she must go and see Duncan for herself, so when her father and Andrew had left she went upstairs to get a jacket. On the way downstairs she looked in Ellen's room. Her sister was lying on the bed reading a book.

'It was silly of you to run away just because Andrew was here,' she said. 'You'll have to meet him some time.'

'Not if I don't want to,' replied Ellen stubbornly, not looking up.

'Once you start going about the glen it'll be difficult to avoid him. He often goes to the hotel and he'll be at the castle on Saturday.'

'Then I'll just have to make sure I don't go to the hotel when he's likely to be there, and I won't go on Saturday to the castle,' replied Ellen smoothly.

'Ach, Ellen, how can you be like that? Nothing can be gained by hiding from him.'

Ellen did not reply and eventually Jan withdrew, frowning with frustration.

Instead of going by way of the Green Gateway she walked up the road and approached the long low cottage along the narrow pathway. As she drew near she could see that the outside of the house had been newly whitewashed and the gleaming paint reflected the golden glow of the afternoon sun and gave the place a serene, well-cared-for look.

She knocked on the door several times, but there was no answer. Wondering if Duncan was busy with an indoor task and had not heard her knocks, she lifted the latch of the door and opened it. Putting her head round it, she called his name. There was no reply.

The smell of new paint inside the house tantalized her and, obeying a strong impulse to see what renovation he had made, she stepped into the main room where she had once drunk tea with Duncan in the smoky gloom of a March afternoon.

The walls of the room had been replastered and were painted a primrose yellow. The floor had been repaired and covered with linoleum tiles. On either side of the re-pointed stone fireplace the two ladderback chairs which her mother had given Duncan were set. They had been scraped and varnished and so had the old table which was still under the window. Instead of a candle in a tin candlestick there was a brand new oil lamp set to one side of a small portable typewriter.

It was the typewriter which held Jan's curious gaze and which drew her slowly towards the table. She stared at it warily as if it was a secret weapon, remembering that Duncan had been carrying a small box in one hand when she had first met him. That box must have contained the typewriter.

Her gaze left it and went to the books which were wedged between two roughly-made wooden book ends at the back of the table. Of its own accord, so it seemed, one of her hands reached out and took one of the books. It was a history of the Highland Clearances which had taken place at the beginning of the nineteenth century.

Flicking the book open, she turned to the front fly-leaf. As she had hoped, a name was scrawled on it. David Garth. Underneath the name an address in the West End of London was written.

Replacing the book, she took out another, also about Scottish history. The same name and address was written in it. A third book told her the same piece of information.

Jan glanced at the sheaf of paper lying beside the type-writer. The pages were covered with typewritten words and she was just about to lift the top page to read it when she felt a shiver go down her spine. She pulled her hand back to her side, aware with a primitive animal-like sensitivity that she was being watched.

She turned quickly. Duncan was standing in the doorway casually leaning against the jamb of the door as he watched her. Across the intervening space she could see that his eyes had a frosty shimmer. No smile softened the firm line of his mouth. His anger at finding her in his house looking at his property was obvious and, knowing herself to be in the wrong, Jan could only stare back at him and wait for that anger to break about her.

# CHAPTER FIVE

'Oh, you startled me! I didn't hear you come in,' exclaimed Jan, taking the initiative as the silence became uncomfortable.

'So I noticed,' he drawled. 'I've been standing here for fully five minutes. I was in the field at the back of the cottage and I saw you arriving. Didn't you hear me calling to you?'

Dumbly she shook her head. The little spurt of courage which had surged her to speak first was fading. If he had been standing there so long he must have seen her reading the fly-leaves of the two books.

He was moving towards her, having closed the door firmly behind him. She was shut into the room with him and he looked distinctly dangerous. Feeling like a trapped animal, she backed away glancing from side to side searching for a way of escape, but there was none, and she eventually found herself backed into the corner of the room beside the table with him standing in front of her his arms folded across his chest. The frosty glint in his eyes made her shiver a little.

'Since I've been living here I've been following the old Highland custom of leaving my front door unlocked so that a passer-by might enter to take shelter or to partake of hospitality,' he said quietly. 'I wasn't aware, however, that there is another custom and that whoever enters the house may abuse the shelter and hospitality by prying and spying amongst the absent host's property.'

Jan stiffened in reaction to his scorn. In all her life no one had ever spoken to her in such a way, but then she had never given anyone reason to do so before.

'I came in because I thought you mightn't have heard me knocking. I wanted to see what you'd done to the inside of the house. I saw the typewriter and the books, so many of them, and ... and ...' She could not go on. The blue eyes were mesmerizing her.

'And that damned curiosity of yours got the better of you,' he grated between taut lips. 'I ought to spank you!'

Shaken by the threat which was uttered with such fervency as if it would give him great pleasure to put her across his knee like a spoilt child and apply his big hand to her bottom, she shrank back against the wall. Then suddenly, resentment that he should think of her and treat as he would treat someone half her age or even younger than that blazed up within her. Liberated by the surge of feeling, she straightened up, determined to show him that she was his equal in spirit if not in physical power. Flinging back her head, she looked him in the eyes again and flared,

'You wouldn't dare, Duncan Davidson! Or should I call you David Garth?'

Only a faint twitch of his eyebrows showed that her accusation had found a mark.

'Oh, I'd dare all right, mate,' he replied coolly. 'Just don't push me too far.'

'David Garth,' she repeated. 'That's your name, isn't it?'

'Let's say it's one of my names,' he countered, still cool.

'Are you a writer?'

'Of sorts.'

'Then why didn't you tell us? What are you trying to hide?' she challenged.

Her challenge seemed to amuse him, although the grin which pulled at one corner of his mouth was rather rueful.

'Apparently very little from you,' he retorted enigmatically. 'Perhaps I should have taken you into my confidence from the first, but it didn't fit with my idea of coming to the glen unknown, a stranger from another land. People wouldn't have reacted naturally if they'd known why I'd come here.'

'I don't understand,' complained Jan.

'I don't expect you to, yet,' he murmured.

The frosty glint had gone from his eyes. His glance lingered thoughtfully on her face as he considered his next move.

'How far can I trust you to keep a secret, Jan?' he queried quietly.

She knew how to keep a secret and had done so many times in the past, for friends. Now the fact that he wanted to trust her made her forget that a few minutes ago she had been afraid of his anger and had wanted to run away from him.

'It depends on how long I have to keep it,' she parried.

'Not long. Until I've done what I came here to do,' he replied.

'And what have you come to do?'

'To write a story and to fulfil a promise. The end of my task is almost in sight. Until then I'd like to stay here and be known as Duncan Davidson.'

'Supposing I can't keep a secret? Supposing I tell everyone in the glen you have been deceiving them. What would you do?' she challenged, not wanting him to think he could get away with his deceit too easily.

He moved a little closer to her, threateningly although amusement glimmered in his face.

'First I would spank you and then I would have to go away without finishing what I came here to do. So you see I'm completely at your mercy. Doesn't that give you a great feeling of power over me?' he said.

She had power over him? Oh no! It was he who had some elusive power over her and he was using it now to defeat her. He was succeeding too. Jan was no longer afraid of what he might do to her. She was afraid of her own reactions to his nearness and she found she was gripping her hands together to prevent them from reaching out to touch him. They wanted to slide up his arms to his shoulders and thence round his neck to tangle in gypsy-black hair.

Although she knew he had given unsatisfactory answers to her accusations and that he did not trust her enough to tell her all about himself, she also knew that she could not let him leave the glen just because she could not keep a secret.

'You can trust me. I won't tell anyone until you say I can,' she replied impulsively, and watched his mouth curve into the smile which jolted her heart, making it skip a beat.

And while that beat was being skipped he leaned forward suddenly and kissed her, gently and gratefully at first, then as her own mouth moved beneath the gentle pressure of his and her hands of their own volition slid up to his shoulders, something strange and beautiful flared between them, and his arms went round her to hold her closely.

'Thanks for the reprieve,' he murmured softly in her ear. He released her to swing away to the hearth and to give the small fire a poke as he hid whatever he might be feeling in performing an ordinary everyday action.

'Now perhaps you'd like to tell me why you've come up here today,' he was saying casually as if nothing of importance had just happened. 'Is your father needing some help?'

'No. I came to make arrangements with you about going to the castle. You'll remember that you've been invited to go with me?'

He turned to look at her, interest glinting in his eyes.

'When?' he asked.

'Tomorrow. The old part of the castle and the gardens will be open to the public. Didn't Sandra tell you when she was here last Friday night?'

He looked puzzled.

'I haven't seen Sandra since the choir practice before last,' he replied. 'And last Friday I wasn't here. I was away all week-end. In fact I didn't come back until yesterday.'

'Oh.' He had been away after all. How had he managed to leave and return without the news of his going and his coming back reverberating through the village? She looked at him with a question in her eyes, but the expression on his face warned her not to ask it. 'But Colin and I passed Sandra in her car on Friday night when we were coming back from a dance in Oban. She was driving very fast, in the same way she was driving the night Chris and I brought Ellen home and saw her coming down the road from here.'

'I can only repeat that she wasn't here last Friday to see me, because I wasn't here. As for the previous week, she didn't come then either. She's never been here.'

Jan stared at him. He returned her gaze directly and steadily and she was sure he was telling the truth.

'Then why has she been driving up and down this road? She must be meeting someone else!' she exclaimed.

'Hasn't it ever occurred to you that there is another car similar to hers in this vicinity and it's that one you and everyone else have been seeing?' he suggested thoughtfully.

'No, it hasn't,' she admitted.

'You've preferred to believe gossip, I suppose,' he remarked with a touch of bitterness. 'But it could be the answer to this particular riddle, and it would also fit in with those suspicions Andrew Forbes has about the poachers.'

'You've seen him, then?'

'In the farmyard this afternoon. He mentioned the matter to me and it was easy to guess he was suspicious of me, or at least someone had suggested to him that I might be involved that same someone who has been trying to get rid of me ever since I came. Any idea who that might be, Bo-Peep?'

Jan kept her eyes averted and looked out of the window at the view down the glen to the distant loch, thinking that anyone who lived in this cottage might come to believe he owned the glen and was lord of all he surveyed, as Hugh MacClachan had once believed.

'No, I haven't,' she mumbled, and wondered unhappily whether Colin had suggested to the factor that Duncan could be the poacher.

Duncan was beside her again and she was tinglingly aware of him, but could not bring herself to look at him.

'Come outside,' he said. 'There's something I want to show you.'

She followed him and outside the house he pointed to tyre marks in the mud of the path.

'There's been a car parked here,' exclaimed Jan.

'Yes, but those marks were not there when I left last Friday morning,' replied Duncan. 'When did it rain last?'

'Wednesday,' said Jan promptly. 'Wednesday night.'

'Then that's when the car was here,' he murmured.

'Sandra could have come up to see if you were home,' she suggested, and he gave her a sardonic glance.

'Too right, mate, she could. But I don't think she did.'

'Then who?'

'Poachers,' he said grimly. 'In a car the same make and colour as Sandra's. It's a fairly common make and colour, as you must know.'

'But what about the other times? Surely you would have heard them.'

'When I'm here a light shows through the window, so they wouldn't park the car close to the house. They'd park it off the road and creep past the house down to the estate. It's easy enough to carry a salmon back up here.

Last week-end and for the last few days they must have noticed that I was away, so they tried for something bigger, being able to park closer.'

'The deer!' exclaimed Jan.

'Exactly. Maybe I ought to start keeping a watch and try to catch them.'

'Oh, Duncan, you'll be careful, please,' she pleaded. 'Sometimes poachers can be violent. They may be tinkers and not mind how they fight.'

'And to think you once compared me to a tinker,' he jeered gently. 'Do you know if there are any about?'

'There are always some about at this time of the year. I believe there are some working on the Robertsons' farm.'

'Where is that?'

'To the north of our land.'

'Then I'll mention it to the factor tomorrow. I suppose he'll be at the castle?'

'Ellen says he will be, so she won't go. She's afraid of meeting him. She thinks he'll be sorry for her because her face is scarred. She can't bear the thought of his pity.'

'What are you going to do about them?' he asked.

Jan looked up at him in surprise, her dark eyes wide.

'I?' she asked. 'What can I do? Ellen won't take any advice from me. You've no idea how stubborn she can be.'

'Oh yes, I have,' he mocked. 'I've met you and the rest of the Reid family, remember. What makes you think she doesn't want him to see her?'

'This afternoon she saw you in the yard. She went out to invite you in for tea because she said it's high time she met you. She came running back when she saw Andrew with Dad and hid in her bedroom until he'd gone.'

He stared at her thoughtfully with narrowed eyes and not for the first time she had the impression that his wits were working swiftly, knowledgeably.

'I think it's also high time this sister of yours and I

met,' he murmured at last. 'I'll come to the farm with you now and persuade her to go with me to the castle tomorrow.'

'Oh, do you think you could?' she exclaimed.

'Yes, I think I could,' he drawled, amusement flickering briefly in his eyes. 'As I see it the job before us tomorrow is to get those two into each other's arms. Don't you agree?'

'Yes, I do,' Jan exclaimed, her eyes shining. 'Then come and meet Ellen now. You could stay for supper.'

'Now, wait a minute. Don't rush me,' he said, half laughing. 'I'm not sure whether I should do that.'

'Why not? It's time you did. Mother's always inviting you and you're always thinking up excuses not to come. I can't think why you won't come.'

'I've always been wary of sitting down to eat in the home of a girl-friend,' he murmured, and she glanced suspiciously at him. Yes, as she'd guessed, he was laughing at her.

'Why?' she asked.

'Because I was once given a warning. It went like this. Never allow yourself to be persuaded to put your knees under the table in the home of a young woman. You'll be at the altar making your vows to her before the year is over if you do.'

'What nonsense!' exclaimed Jan.

'It isn't nonsense at all. I can assure you I've had some very narrow escapes,' he replied wryly.

'Well, you needn't worry about Ellen or me. She loves Andrew even though she won't admit she does, and I . . .' Once again she couldn't continue, because of the way he was looking at her.

'And you, Jan?' he prompted curiously. 'Do you love someone?'

She became very interested suddenly in the tyre marks pushing at the dried mud with the toe of her brogue, not wishing to face that intense blue gaze.

'O.K.,' he drawled. 'None of my business. Since you say I've nothing to fear I'll come to supper to meet Ellen. Hang on for a minute while I change into a clean shirt and wash my hands.'

He went into the cottage and Jan waited in the mellow sunshine, thinking of the name she had seen written on the fly-leaf of a book. David Garth. A secret she had promised to keep. A promise she would not break. She had already received her reward in the form of a kiss – a kiss which had taught her more about herself than anything else that had happened to her. The lines of the poem by Burns sang through her mind; words written about another Duncan Davidson: 'A man may kiss a bonnie lass, And ay be welcome back again!' Duncan had kissed her the day they had gone to Oban. Today he had kissed her again and he had shown him that he was very welcome. Had she shown him too much?

He reappeared and closed the cottage door after him. They set off in the direction of Bealach Glas, skirting round the potato field to reach it.

As she waited for Duncan to close the gate after she had gone through it on to the patch of emerald green grass, Jan gazed down over the fields to the loch which was shimmering under the tranquil golden light of the sun. Unaware of the pleasure expressed on her face, she started when Duncan said,

'You couldn't live anywhere else, could you?'

She flicked a glance in his direction. He was looking very serious.

'I would find it difficult,' she replied carefully.

'Even if you were living with someone you loved?' he queried. 'Even if you could come back occasionally and visit the glen?'

She was reminded of what she had said to Ellen earlier in the afternoon about loving a person sufficiently to come to a compromise with him, and realized that it was one thing to hand out advice but quite another to take the same advice herself. Could she give up living in the glen to be with someone she loved? Could she ever love anyone that much?

She looked into intensely blue eyes which were watching her closely and found the answer to her question. If Duncan asked her to go away with him she would go without a backward glance and follow him to the ends of the earth!

'I gather from your silence that you won't even consider the matter,' he said suddenly and rather harshly, jolting her out of her musings.

'I'd have to love someone very much before I could leave,' she stammered. 'And he would have to have a lot of love to offer me. You said once that you valued your freedom and that a woman would have to have a lot to offer you before you could stay and live where she lived. The same applies to me the other way round.'

They gazed at each other searchingly, measuringly, standing on the thick green grass in the golden light of early evening. A curlew cried and three ducks flew hurriedly in strict V-formation down river towards the loch.

'I think we'd better move on,' said Duncan, turning away to suit his action to his words. 'This gateway is not to be trusted.'

There was a lightness in his voice which deliberately mocked their recent conversation and Jan followed him in silence down to the farmhouse, feeling disillusion seep into her mind.

At Tighnacoarach the table was set already for supper, but Duncan was made welcome. Ellen came into the room and her ravaged face, still pale and troubled after seeing Andrew unexpectedly, lit up when she saw that they had a visitor and within a short time Duncan had charmed her out of her defensive mood and she was chatting to him as if he were an old friend. The evening passed pleasantly and by the time Duncan left Ellen had agreed to go to the castle the next day.

Early on Saturday afternoon Duncan drove Sheena's car down the glen to the village and on to the ferry. The waters of the loch were calm, shading from violet-grey to deep olive green where trees crowded to its edge to admire their reflections.

Sitting in the back seat of the car listening to Ellen talking happily to Duncan about her acting career, Jan could not help wishing that she and Duncan were alone going on an outing together as they had gone that bright and beautiful May day when life had been so simple and uncomplicated.

The gardens at Dunmore were known throughout the country for the variety of plants grown there, so it was not surprising that the courtyard in front of the castle was crammed with cars. Pale sunlight breaking through the thin grey cloud glinted on the greenish-grey granite of the old castle tower, softening the grim aspect which the ancient stronghold of the MacClachans normally presented to the world.

Jan had hardly stepped from the car when Colin seemed to pounce on her from nowhere. Grasping her by the hand, he pulled her over to the shrubbery of huge rhododendron bushes, towers of green leaves which edged the courtyard.

'I've remembered,' said Colin in a fierce whisper as he glanced warily at Duncan who was locking the doors of the car.

'Remembered what?' demanded Jan, freeing herself from his grasp.

'Where I saw the portrait of the man who looks like him,' he replied, jerking his head in the direction of Duncan who with Ellen was walking off in the opposite direction.

'Where?' asked Jan, impatient now.

'Here.'

'In the castle?' she squeaked incredulously.

'No, not exactly. I mean I didn't see it *in* the castle itself, but in the stable. Come and let me show you.'

She followed him along the path which wound through the shrubbery to the outbuildings behind the three-storeyed gabled-ended house.

'In here,' said Colin, pushing open the door of the lowest building. Inside was dim and Jan could just make out the old stall where horses had once stood and which were now filled with discarded furniture. Against one wall some old picture frames were stacked.

'When Sandra was eighteen she had a birthday party to which I was invited. I think possibly Ellen was too,' explained Colin excitedly. 'We played a kind of sophisticated hide-and-seek game. Instead of one person seeking and the rest hiding it was the other way round. One person hid and the rest looked for her. Sandra, as you can guess, hid in here. Up in the hay loft, as a matter of fact.' He pointed to the trapdoor in the ceiling of the stable.

'Now the idea was when you found the person who was hiding you stayed hidden with her until the next person came along and found you,' continued Colin, 'and this went on until everyone was squashed into the hiding place.'

'I remember playing it once,' said Jan with a laugh. 'We used to call it Sardines because we all had to squash into a small space like sardines in a tin.'

'That's it,' replied Colin with a grin. 'It used to be a good excuse for putting your arm around a lass and squeezing her.'

'Is that what you did to Sandra when you found her?' she teased. 'You were the first to find her, weren't you?'

'Never you mind,' he retorted, although she had the impression her taunt disturbed him. 'Before I found her I had a look at the pictures which were stacked in there, and it was then I saw The Chieftain. I came face to face with him suddenly. It gave me a shock, so it did, to find him staring at me so disdainfully. Now you'll see that there are still some pictures here, but he isn't amongst them. I've looked this afternoon. None of the portraits which were here then are here now.'

Jan went over to the dusty frames and examined the pictures. They were mostly sepia engravings of Highland cattle grazing in dim glens or of red deer poised warily on rocks near tumbling waterfalls.

'How disappointing,' she said. 'Perhaps they've been sold.'

'Perhaps,' said Colin. 'But I've been thinking. You're on good terms with Mrs. Lang. You could ask her where they've gone when you see her.'

'I suppose I could. You're quite sure you saw the portrait here?'

'Of course I am,' he replied testily. 'I was thinking about that party and about being hidden in the loft for nearly half an hour with Sandra before anyone found us, when it came to me in a flash where I'd seen the portrait, so I came straight to the stable to see if it was still here.'

'Maybe that's why Sandra thinks she'd seen Duncan somewhere too,' said Jan excitedly. 'She would know of the portrait too, wouldn't she?'

'I expect so,' he muttered.

'Then why don't you ask her where it is?'

'I will if I find myself anywhere near her today. Let's go and look at the gardens now.'

The gardens, which had been developed by Cameron Lang, the Colonel's father, were adjacent to the loch, the shores of which were washed by the warm and beneficial Gulf Stream which brings mild weather to the coasts of Britain. They were enclosed on three sides by high stone walls. The fourth side running parallel to the loch was bounded by a thick hawthorn hedge.

From a central gravel path long broad grass walks radiated outwards and from them narrow paths bordered by shrubs led to small secret gardens, each one a different delight. There were small lawns dotted with blossom trees and edged with perennial plants. There was the pond garden where swathes of golden senecio overhung a still pool on which waterlily pads floated. There was a rose garden, an aromatic garden and a rock garden where numerous tiny plants clung to well arranged boulders. And everywhere there were people enjoying a Saturday afternoon stroll in the mild sunshine.

It was not until they entered the humid warmth of the circular greenhouse with its dome of glass, where begonias and fuchsia bloomed in profusion and the leaves of orange and grapefruit trees drooped gracefully over all, that they met anyone they knew. Sandra was there, stunning in a simple white tweed skirt and bouclé jumper, a glowing silk scarf knotted with casual elegance round her neck. She was talking pleasantly to a group of people, but when she saw Jan and Colin enter she excused herself and came across to them.

'I'm so glad to see you,' she said to Jan. 'Where's Duncan? Has he come?'

'He's with Ellen somewhere,' replied Jan.

A frown pleated tiny lines between Sandra's finely arched eyebrows.

'I must go and look for him. Tea is being served at four in the banqueting hall at the old castle,' she said. Her white teeth gnawed briefly at her lower lip as she gave Colin a strange sidelong glance. 'You'll show Jan where that is, I hope. Do you remember it?'

'I've forgotten nothing,' he replied coolly, returning her glance frankly, and to Jan's surprise Sandra's eyelids drooped over her green eyes and faint pink colour appeared in her cheeks. 'I also remember some portraits which were in the stable. They were there when we played Sardines at your birthday party. Do you remember?' added Colin.

Colour glowed even more hotly in Sandra's cheeks and her glance was startled as she looked at him. Jan had the oddest feeling that she might as well have not been there for all the notice the other two were taking of her. They seemed to be in a trance.

Voices of newcomers to the greenhouse broke the silence and brought an end to the trance. Sandra's eyes flickered and were veiled again by the bronze-coloured lashes.

'Yes, I remember,' she said in a rather strained voice.

'They aren't there now,' said Colin matter-of-factly, although his heightened colour showed that he too was affected by this meeting. 'Do you know where they are now?'

'They're in the castle. Daddy had them restored and hung in the gallery there. It overlooks the banqueting hall,' replied Sandra breathlessly. 'You should go and see it. It's been restored perfectly and must look just as it did before the Forty-Five rebellion. Excuse me now. I must go and look for Duncan. And for Ellen, too,' she added as an afterthought. 'Mother asked me to take them to her as soon as they arrived, but I missed them.'

She went out of the greenhouse quickly and Colin watched her go with a slight frown on his face.

'Do you know, that's the first time she's spoken to me for years. Looks as if a little competition isn't doing her any harm at all,' he murmured.

'What competition?' asked Jan innocently, and he glanced at her.

'Ellen making off with your crofter friend,' he said. 'And now for the gallery in the banqueting hall to see if The Chieftain is lurking there. Come on.'

A little disturbed by his suggestion about Ellen and Duncan, Jan followed him out of the greenhouse. Back along the gravel path they went through the gateway to the courtyard in front of the castle.

At the entrance to the tower Colin had a few words with the Langs' butler Hector Dobie, who was a member of the choir, and he showed them the way to a small door in a thick stone wall which, when opened, revealed a narrow winding flight of stairs leading up to the gallery from which they were able to look down into the banqueting hall below.

As Sandra had said, the restoration of the hall had been perfectly carried out. The greenish-grey granite of the walls had been hung with old tapestries depicting hunting scenes and from the dark rafters of the roof wrought-iron chandeliers hung. For this afternoon's tea the long refectory table had been covered with white cloths and set with crockery and plates of cakes and biscuits.

'There he is. Look!' exclaimed Colin triumphantly.

Jan turned and looked. At one end of the gallery was a huge portrait of a man in Highland dress. Following Colin, she went and stood in front of it and stared.

The red and blue tartan of his kilt and plaid proclaimed to Jan at once that he was a MacClachan, and she felt excitement stir within her. Slowly she let her gaze travel upwards over the painted sporran, with its tassels of fur, to the graceful hand which rested on the hilt of a sword; up over the diamond-shaped buttons of a velvet jacket to the big brooch, Celtic in design, which held the plaid in place at his shoulder; up to a rounded stubborn chin, a firm straight mouth, a curved dominant nose, haughty eyebrows, gypsy-black hair tied at the neck and back to eyes which gazed down at her disdainfully. They weren't blue. They were black.

She was aware that Colin was waiting almost avidly for her reaction.

'Well? What do you think?' he demanded. 'Isn't he like Davidson?'

'There are resemblances. At first glance he could be Duncan, but looking more closely I can see many differences. His chin is a different shape and his eyes are a different colour,' murmured Jan, more shaken than she wanted to admit by the picture.

'Aye, I daresay there are differences if you care to look for them. I wouldn't be knowing the colour of Davidson's eyes myself,' said Colin dryly. 'I haven't been that close to him. But there's likeness enough to make anyone think they could be related, isn't there?'

'I suppose so,' admitted Jan reluctantly.

'Let's see if they've decided who he is,' said Colin, and leaning forward he peered at the inscription under the painting.

'Hugh MacClachan, sixteenth chief of that clan. He was killed at the Battle of Culloden and his lands were seized as attained and eventually sold to David Duncan who became the laird of Dunmore,' Colin read aloud. 'So that's who he is. It's going to be interesting to see the reaction of the Colonel when he comes face to face with Duncan Davidson . . .' His voice trailed away and he leaned forward again to read the inscription under the picture, and Jan could see him mouthing the words silently as the same thought occurred to him that had occurred to her.

'David Duncan. Duncan Davidson,' he said slowly, and glanced at her, his eyes bright with excitement. 'Are you thinking what I'm thinking? Or is it too much of a coincidence?'

'I don't know,' mumbled Jan, who was thinking of that other name, David Garth. 'It's very strange. Are all the portraits up here of members of the MacClachan family?'

'I shouldn't think so. They're more likely to be Duncans. Let's have a look at them.'

Slowly they paced down both sides of the gallery, gazing at the painted faces of men women and children. Some of the portraits were good, but most of them were very poor, showing wooden-looking people with lacklustre eyes. It wasn't until they reached the opposite end of the gallery to the portrait of The Chieftain that they noticed a picture which looked as if it had been painted by an artist who had possessed a gift for making his subject look lifelike.

It showed a man with two women, one of whom was obviously his wife, the other, much younger, probably being his daughter. The eyes of the man and of the young woman caught Jan's attention. They were blue, the sapphire blue of the loch on a cold sunny day. She went back to read the inscription beneath the picture. It told her that the man was Gilbert Duncan, laird of Dunmore, that the older woman was his wife Jean and that the younger women was his daughter Fiona.

Fiona Duncan, who had married Hugh MacClachan and whose son Davey had had blue eyes and black hair.

She glanced again at the painted face of the younger woman. It was pretty and wilful, crowned by the tumbling glory of masses of golden hair. The glance of the blue eyes was cool and tantalizing and the curve of the beautiful mouth was passionate. It wasn't difficult to imagine such a person eloping in defiance of her parents with a black-haired, black-eyed rogue, who had borne the same name as the long-dead chief of the MacClachan clan.

'I'll have to bring Duncan up here to show him the portrait,' said Jan as she followed Colin down the winding stairs.

'That should be easy enough. When we're having tea you detach him from your sister while I keep her busy talking.'

In the banqueting hall Mrs. Lang greeted them graciously, saying she was pleased to see Colin again and asking for Ellen and Duncan.

'They're just coming in now, Mrs. Lang,' said Colin.

Ellen and Duncan were apparently too engrossed in each other to realize that Mrs. Lang was waiting to talk to them, so Jan offered to go and bring them over to her. As she worked her way through the groups of chattering people she saw Andrew enter the room. He looked around, saw Ellen talking to Duncan, and a strange, almost vicious expression passed over his craggy features.

Slowly he began to make his way towards the couple, arriving beside them at the same time as Jan.

Jan moved forward quickly, obeying her instinct. She touched Duncan on the arm. He turned to look down at her.

'I've something to show you,' she whispered. 'It's in the portrait gallery.'

Out of the corner of her eyes she saw Ellen raise a hand to her face to hide the scar from Andrew, who had swung her round to face him.

Interest glimmered in Duncan's eyes, but he hesitated.

'Can't it wait?' he asked. 'I was just going to tell the factor about my theory concerning the poachers.'

'You'll not be doing that now,' said Jan urgently. 'Look at them. We'd best be leaving them alone.'

Duncan looked in the direction she was looking. Andrew was staring at Ellen as if he had never seen her before and she was staring back at him, her eyes wide above her shielding hand. Andrew reached out and pulled Ellen's hand gently away from her face and for the first time Jan saw emotion thrust aside his habitual non-committal expression as his mouth lost its stern line and his eyes darkened and narrowed in pain. Then still holding Ellen's hand he led her out of the room, winding through the groups of people, taking her through one of the sturdy nail-decorated oak doors out into the courtyard.

Duncan turned and gave Jan a kindly conspiratorial look which made her want suddenly to hug him.

'It worked!' he grinned. 'My attentions to Ellen during the afternoon seemed to have roused the sleeping tiger in the factor. We've been dodging him round hedges and tree trunks, always managing to avoid meeting him face to face. Looks as if competition woke him up, and now possibly he'll go into action.'

Just then they noticed Sandra making her way towards them with a determined expression on her face.

'And perhaps you were hoping there would be some action from another person too,' she remarked rather tartly.

Duncan chuckled as he also noticed Sandra.

'We were dodging her too,' he murmured, then added rather mischievously, deliberately turning his back on Sandra, 'What is it you want to show me?'

'The portrait that Colin said was like you. It's up there in the gallery. Come on, before Sandra reaches us,' urged Jan.

But going out of the hall they met the Colonel coming in. An erect spare man with iron-grey hair and a bristling military moustache, he recognized Jan at once and greeted her with a smile. His glance went to Duncan. His smile vanished and was replaced by an expression of incredulity which was almost identical to the expression which had chased across Mrs. Lang's face when Sandra had introduced her to Duncan in the lobby of the hotel in Oban.

'Good lord!' gasped the Colonel, his hand going to the top pocket of his tweed jacket to take out his glasses. He put them on and peered at Duncan. 'Who the devil are you?' he rapped.

'This is Duncan Davidson, Daddy. You remember Mummy and me telling you about him.' Sandra had caught up with them and was standing on the other side of Duncan pushing a possessive arm through his, smiling up at him as if she also shared a secret with him. 'He's living in that old croft on the far side of the estate.'

'Ah, yes, I remember.' The Colonel was recovering his poise and holding out his hand. 'How do you do. You're from Down Under, I hear, and want to trace your ancestors. Davidson, eh? Afraid you're in the wrong territory. That clan was more over to the north-east of the country. Sure it's your name?'

He was staring at Duncan again as if he couldn't believe his eyes. Duncan glanced sideways at Jan and winked as he drawled,

'No, as a matter of fact I'm not sure what my family name is.'

'Oh, Duncan, how can you possibly hope to trace your ancestors if you're not sure of your family name?' exclaimed Sandra, who was obviously unpleasantly surprised by his admission.

'It will make tracing them difficult,' said the Colonel in his abrupt clipped way, suddenly very authoritative as if he felt his ability to trace someone's ancestry was being challenged by his daughter. 'But it isn't necessary to know the family name, because you may have other information we can follow up. For instance, which part of Australia do you come from?'

Duncan seemed to hesitate. He looked from the Colonel to Sandra, then back again. A faintly mocking smile hovered about his mouth as he said,

'I was born at a place called Cobarmulla in New South Wales,' he murmured.

'Good lord!' exclaimed the Colonel again. 'I've been there. Actually stayed on a huge sheep station there for a few days. It belonged to a chap called Bennett. I was absolutely fascinated by the place. I couldn't help comparing the set-up with the medieval communities which used to exist in this country. Rather feudal, you know. The station owner was like the squire or laird used to be here, responsible for the welfare of all the people on the station. The only difference, of course, was that on a station everyone is equal and there is no touching of the forelock or bending of the knee, but I felt that the station owner's word was law. You'll know what I'm talking about, I daresay.'

The Colonel cocked a sharp eye at Duncan, who replied calmly,

'I believe I do.'

'Yes, well – er – let me see,' continued the Colonel. 'Having established where you were born I think the next step would be for us to find out if anyone who emigrated from here went to that part of Australia and follow it from there. Have you any idea what occupation your father followed?'

'I believe he was a roustabout.'

'Hmm. That isn't an easy one to follow, because they have a way of moving from station to station. What about your paternal grandfather now?'

'He could have been a sheep-shearer.'

The Colonel sighed and shook his head.

'That's difficult, very difficult, because they're a wandering tribe too.'

He peered closely at Duncan again, then glanced around the room. He removed his glasses, put them in their case and placed it in his jacket pocket. 'I'd like to have a word in private, young man. Your case interests me for a variety of reasons. Supposing we go along to my study now? There's a rather personal aspect of the whole affair which I'd like to discuss. Have you time?'

'Yes, I've time.'

'Right. Then come along with me.'

'Shall I tell Mummy we'll be having another guest to supper tonight?' asked Sandra.

'That might be a good idea,' said the Colonel briskly. 'Are you agreeable, Davidson?'

'Thank you,' said Duncan smoothly, and added for Jan's ears only, 'I'll find my own way home.'

'Remember the warning about not getting your knees under the table,' she whispered, and he gave her a thoughtful glance.

'Not to worry, mate. It doesn't apply this time.'

What had he meant by that? Jan wondered. Had he meant that the warning didn't apply in the case of him sitting down at the meal table in Sandra's home because he loved Sandra and wanted to marry her?

She decided that was so and also that the relationship between his daughter and Duncan was the personal matter which the Colonel had wished to discuss.

Left alone in the almost empty banqueting hall where Hector Dobie and his staff were clearing away the empty plates and cups and saucers, she felt let-down and deserted. As she stepped out into the courtyard she wondered where she should look for Ellen so that they could go home.

'Sorry I wasn't able to help at the crucial moment.' Colin was beside her, a little breathless. 'I couldn't get away from Mrs. Lang. What's happened to Davidson? Did you show him the portrait?'

'I didn't get the chance. We met the Colonel, who's taken him off to his study. He wants to help Duncan trace his ancestors. I think Duncan is going to ask the Colonel if he can marry Sandra,' said Jan in a flat monotone, saying what was uppermost in her mind.

'What?' Colin almost shouted, and people who were just getting into the cars to leave turned to look at him curiously. Aware of their interest, he took Jan's arm.

'Let's go somewhere quiet where we can talk,' he muttered, and once again Jan found herself in the walled gardens. He took her to the rose garden and they sat on the white-painted Regency cast-iron seat for two, the feet of which were hidden in a clump of foaming *alchemilla mollia* and was shaded by rambling roses which climbed up a green trellis.

'Now what makes you think that Duncan is going to ask the Colonel if he can marry Sandra?' demanded Colin. 'Has he proposed to her?'

'I don't know. He may have done. He's going to stay to supper with the Langs. He didn't hesitate about accepting the invitation.'

'What's that got to do with it?' rapped Colin rather impatiently.

She told him about the warning Duncan had once been given about not getting his knees under the table at the home of a girl-friend if he didn't want to marry her and how he had always resisted invitations to the Reids' house for a meal.

'A ridiculous idea, but I see what you mean,' muttered Colin, frowning. 'He didn't hesitate because he doesn't mind getting his knees under that particular table because he wouldn't mind marrying Sandra. You know, it's a pity you weren't able to show him the portrait, because I was hoping that once he'd seen that he'd have the decency to clear out of the glen.'

Jan rounded on him in bewilderment.

'You're making as much sense as I am. Why should he leave the glen just because he resembles the portrait?'

'Not any portrait,' he reminded her. 'But the portrait of the last chief of the MacClachans, the family which by rights should own all this.' He waved his hand in a gesture which took in the gardens and the castle walls. 'Mrs. Lang has just been telling me that her father-in-law had those portraits removed when he inherited the castle because he didn't like to be reminded that but for the act of attainder which took the estate from the MacClachans the Duncans would never have owned it, and that means that Cameron Lang would never have inherited.'

'Nor would he have inherited if Davey MacClachan had been found,' murmured Jan, thinking of an old sheep-shearer who could have been Duncan's grandfather; of the expressions of incredulity on Colonel's and Mrs. Lang's faces when they had come face to face with Duncan; of the eagerness of the Colonel to discuss a personal matter with Duncan in private.

'I'm glad you see the point I'm trying to make,' said Colin dryly.

'Perhaps the Colonel will show the portrait to Duncan,' she said hopefully, 'and then he'll leave the glen,' she added, and the tone of her voice changed woefully at the thought of Duncan leaving the glen.

'And perhaps he won't,' muttered Colin miserably.

'Why do you dislike him so much?' challenged Jan once again.

'I don't dislike him, but I wish he'd never come here. Can't you see that by coming when he did he fouled everything up?'

'In what way?'

Colin was silent for a few minutes, staring morosely at the summer swallows which were swooping and twittering about the garden enjoying the mellow warmth of the afternoon sunshine.

'There was just a chance, admittedly a rather slight one, that if Duncan hadn't turned up in the glen when he did Sandra might have been glad to have found an old friend like myself here and have turned to me,' Colin said musingly.

'But you told me you'd got over your infatuation.'

'I said that to cover up what I was really feeling on seeing her hobnobbing with a handsome stranger. I tried to pretend I didn't care, that I'd found someone else, you in fact, to take her place. But every week when I've seen them together at choir practice I've writhed inside with envy and I've looked for ways to get rid of him, by making him unpopular here.'

'So it was you who encouraged the gossip,' accused Jan.

His grin was a little shamefaced.

'And suggested to Andrew Forbes that Duncan might be the poacher he was looking for,' he admitted.

'Ach, Colin, how could you?' she exclaimed.

'When you see what you want most in the world being filched from beneath your very nose there aren't any lengths you'll go to to prevent the robbery from taking place,' he muttered dourly. 'Then when I saw the portrait this afternoon I had another idea. I thought that if some relationship to the MacClachans could be established that might put the Colonel on the look-out. It wouldn't be wise for Sandra to marry the grandson of Davey MacClachan, who was first cousin to her own grandfather, would it?'

'So you think he might be related to Davey too?' said Jan, surprised.

'Everyone in the district who's over eighty years of age and who's seen Duncan thinks that,' he muttered morosely.

'Well, that doesn't make many people,' replied Jan.

'Four, to be exact. Your grandmother, my grandfather, Hector Dobie's Aunt Maggie and Hamish Grant's father. They all went to the village school when there was one and so did Davey MacClachan. They all remember him. They've all seen Duncan and say he's very like him.'

'Then why haven't you told Duncan this?'

'Because I didn't really believe any of them at first. I know that old folks' memories often play tricks on them and I decided that just because Duncan's colouring was similar to that of Davey and he happened to come from Australia, they were romancing about him. Now I've seen the portrait again I'm beginning to think that there might be something in what they say.'

'But there's no real proof,' said Jan.

'How do we know that there isn't? Who knows what the Colonel has in his study which he's turning over now?' he argued. 'I'm also willing to bet that Duncan had a good idea that he might be a descendant of the man in the portrait when he came here, and that's why he chose this particular glen.'

Jan sat silent. Colin was only putting into words her own thoughts and fancies about Duncan. But she didn't feel very happy about it. She had an odd uneasy feeling that there was tragedy inherent in Colin's suggestions. Supposing it was proved beyond a shadow of doubt that Duncan was not only a MacClachan but also the grandson of David MacClachan who had gone to Australia, it would mean that he and Sandra were very closely related and possibly should not marry; and since by now they were probably very much in love with each other it was going to cause them a great deal of unhappiness.

On the other hand there was Colin, so much in love with Sandra even after all these years that he was prepared to do anything to make Duncan leave the glen and prevent him from marrying Sandra.

Jan sighed in a perplexed fashion and Colin gave her an amused glance as he rose to his feet.

'There's nothing more we can do except wait. I'm going home now. I'll see you in church tomorrow, I expect.'

She went with him back to the courtyard. All the cars except theirs had gone.

'I'll have to find Ellen,' said Jan. 'I wonder where she's gone.'

'Probably to Andrew's cottage. I shouldn't bother them just now,' he remarked with a knowing grin. 'He'll take her home.'

He drove off and while she was hesitating debating whether to drive to Andrew's cottage to look for her sister or not, Sandra came running out of the front door of the white house. She stopped short and looked round.

'Oh, bother. Has Colin gone?' she exclaimed. 'I've been looking for him everywhere. Where were you both?'

'In the rose garden.'

'How romantic,' jeered Sandra. 'You should be careful. He may not look it, but he's a bit of a wolf. I've reason to know, remembering how he behaved that time we hid in the loft in the stables.'

'Was it because of what happened there that you haven't spoken to him for years until today?' asked Jan curiously.

Sandra's eyes opened wide and an expression of annoyance crossed her face.

'Did he dare to tell you what happened there?' she demanded.

'No, not exactly. He just said that you hadn't spoken to him for years. He didn't say why.'

An expression of relief on Sandra's face was followed by one of embarrassment.

'I haven't had much chance to speak to him,' she said defensively. 'I was sent away to Switzerland after that party. Sometimes I think my parents sent me away deliberately in the hopes I'd have nothing more to do with Colin. I always hoped he would write to me, but he didn't, and gradually I came to the conclusion that he hadn't been serious when he'd kissed me in the loft. I was very hurt. You know how foolish and vulnerable you are when you're eighteen. You fall in love and when you find that your love isn't returned you think the end of the world has come.' She stopped speaking, aware perhaps that she was saying too much about herself. Shaking her hair back, she added lightly, 'I made darned sure I wasn't going to be hurt in that way again. That's why I stayed down in London when I came back from Switzerland, to have lots of fun.'

'And to get engaged to the Honourable James,' said Jan. 'Was that fun?'

'Don't be beastly, Jan Reid,' retorted Sandra, making a face. 'No, it wasn't. He was far too old for me. I'm so glad he realized that too. Are you going home now?'

'I expect so.'

'It's a pity Colin has gone. I'll have to ring him up. Perdito, that's our poodle, you know, has just been sick all over the drawing-room carpet. Mother thinks it may have eaten something it shouldn't have. 'Bye.'

Sandra swung away and started towards the house, remembered something and turned back to call with a smile,

'Thanks for bringing Duncan with you. Daddy is quite fascinated by him. It's terribly exciting.'

She ran into the house and Jan got into the car, started it up and drove away down the driveway, her mind buzzing with all that she had learned that afternoon.

Colin admitting that he was in love with Sandra and

that he would do anything to make Duncan leave the glen. Sandra saying that she had fallen in love with Colin when she was eighteen and had been hurt when he hadn't written to her. Why hadn't he written? Had Sandra's parents intercepted any correspondence between the two young people as part of their efforts to nip any love affair between them in the bud?

Poor Sandra. Poor Colin. Jan's generous impulsive heart went out to them. To think that their love might have been re-kindled and might even now have been progressing towards a happy ending if Duncan hadn't appeared on the scene and caught Sandra's attention.

If Duncan could be persuaded to leave the glen soon, possibly tomorrow, Colin might still have a chance!

The idea seemed to come from nowhere and grew and grew in her mind. Ignoring the pain which the thought of Duncan's departure brought to herself, Jan applied her ingenuity to the matter with enthusiasm. But by the time she reached Tighnacoarach only one way had suggested itself to her. She and she alone could put Duncan in a position that would lead to his departure. She could tell everyone that he was not Duncan Davidson but David Garth. She could break her promise to keep his secret!

Chris was in the kitchen of the farmhouse, an unusual occurrence for a Saturday afternoon which was often busy at the hotel this time of the year. She had come in a state of excitement to tell them about some people who had arrived in the village that afternoon.

When Jan walked in Chris stopped speaking to ask,

'Is Duncan with you?'

'No. He's still at the castle discussing something with the Colonel.'

Chris nodded, her dark eyes glinting knowingly as if she knew all about Duncan and the Colonel and their subject of discussion.

'Aye, he would have to be approached before anything could be done,' she said in a way which caused them all to stare at her.

'Before what could be done?' demanded Sheena. 'Ach, Chris, you're that irritating! You're just trying to whet our appetites with your remarks. Now stop your teasing and tell us what you know.'

'It's so exciting I don't know where to begin to tell you,' said Chris.

'You've been beginning for the past ten minutes,' commented John Reid, at his driest. 'And all we know so far is that five strangers, one with a beard and a lot of hair, appeared at the hotel this afternoon and started asking a lot of questions. Now instead of trying to describe each one of them in detail why don't you tell us why they're here?'

'All right, I will,' said Chris. Then taking a deep breath she announced importantly, 'They're making a film and the glen is going to be in it.'

'What sort of film?' asked Sheena.

'I expect it'll be one of those nature films,' said John. 'I mind someone did one about a Hebridean island for the television. It was after showing the way of life of the people and the geology and plant life. I mind it was very good in its way. There were some fine photographs of the hills and glens and the birds.'

Agnes Reid made no comment on Chris's announcement, but rocked back and forth, her misty grey eyes empty and staring.

'No, it won't be a nature film. But it is for television,' said Chris importantly. 'It's a story, partly fact and partly fiction, so they were telling me. The glen will be shown only in the last instalment which isn't written yet.'

'What is the story about?' asked Sheena.

'About the descendant of an emigrant Highlander. The film will show him tracing the way back to Scotland, following in reverse the way his ancestor took until he reaches the glen where the actual emigrant was born,' replied Chris, and Jan felt a strange chill creeping over her body.

'To write about the glen someone would have to live here and know all about it,' objected Sheena sharply. 'Who is writing it?'

'A man called David Garth. He's done several scripts for documentary travel films. They say he's been living in the glen for some weeks now.'

'But there's no one of that name here,' exclaimed Sheena.

'It's not like you to miss the point,' scoffed John softly, and Sheena turned to look at him and then back at Chris, trying to read the expressions on their faces, while Jan felt thankful that she wouldn't have to break her promise to Duncan after all.

'Ach, you must be pulling my leg,' said Sheena at last. 'You're never meaning that Duncan Davidson is this David Garth you're talking about?'

# CHAPTER SIX

THE short sharp silence which followed Sheena's exclamation was broken first by Agnes Reid.

'I knew fine he wasn't a Duncan or a Davidson,' she intoned as she rocked back and forth in her chair, her eyes wide and staring. 'He's David Maclachan, with his hair the colour of jet and his eyes as blue as periwinkles.'

'Garth, not MacClachan,' said Sheena irritably. 'Ach, you've got the MacClachans on the brain, Mother.'

'And I knew very well that there was more to him than met the eye,' murmured John. 'No roustabout ever knew as much about the Highland Clearances as he does or was so knowledgeable about the rest of the country's history. He's done his work well, whoever he is. Did they tell you when they plan to do the filming?'

'I expect they'd like to do it during the next month or so while the weather is good, but first of all they have to have permission from the Colonel to photograph the castle. I expect that's why Duncan, I mean David – ach, it's going to be difficult calling him by another name – I expect that's why he's at the castle now seeing the Colonel.'

'It doesn't bear thinking about,' exclaimed Sheena suddenly, her dark eyes flashing. 'We've had a real live writer living in the house next door, you might say, for nearly three months and we've not known it. Just wait until I see that long devil! I'll give him a piece of my mind. You'd have thought he could have told us who he is and why he is here. Ach, the deceiving ways of him, and me letting him persuade me into giving him those chairs.'

'Now, now, lass, I'm not having that,' put in John. 'You know very well you insisted on him having them. You didn't give him a chance to refuse them?'

Sheena swung round to confront him.

'You're making it sound as if he didn't want the dratted things,' she countered.

'Well, did he?' he retorted, his eyes beginning to twinkle as he teased her, and although she tossed her head so that her wiry white-sprinkled black hair bounced her grin appeared.

'Perhaps he didn't,' she admitted. 'But why didn't he tell us he's a writer?'

'Imagine what would have happened if he had,' murmured Chris, rolling her eyes expressively. 'We'd have either treated him as if he was some strange god to be worshipped from afar or regarded him with even more suspicion than we did.'

'If we'd known he was here looking for local colour we'd have all behaved like hedgehogs,' put in Jan, who was suddenly understanding several remarks Duncan had made. 'As it was he came just as anyone wanting to settle in the glen might have come and we treated him accordingly. We behaved naturally, but we wouldn't have done if we'd known he was watching us closely.'

'I suppose you're right,' sighed Sheena, giving her youngest daughter a sharp appraising glance. 'Did he ever mention his writing to you?'

'No, although like Dad I couldn't help thinking he wasn't a simple odd job man.'

'I wonder why he picked this particular glen,' mused Chris thoughtfully.

'He chose it because he belongs here,' sighed Agnes, who was still looking vacant and dreamy. 'He's a Mac-Clachan, and it's his glen as much as it's mine and more than it's yours. The MacClachans fought the Robertsons for it. They bought it with their blood and no matter how far any of them have strayed away from it they will keep returning until one day there is a MacClachan back in the castle. Didn't Hugh MacClachan, the last chief, say before he died of his wounds on the battlefield at Culloden that his blood was strong and as long as it flowed in the veins of his descendants they would keep trying to come back to the glen? Yon lad is living proof that the blood is strong.'

'And that the heart is Highland,' added Jan softly.

'Ach, how can you keep saying he's a MacClachan when his name is Garth?' argued Sheena impatiently, not in the least impressed by her mother-in-law's fancies.

'Maybe his mother was a MacClachan,' said Chris brightly. 'After all, we women do have our uses. We can pass on blood and heart just as well as any man.'

'The only thing that is certain is that he has come from Australia,' said John. 'And I'm willing to believe that he's been in Nova Scotia and British Columbia too. He's been very particular in collecting information for the script and I expect that's why he got the commission to write it. And I can't help feeling relieved that we know who he is and why he's come here. Did you not bring Ellen back with you, Jan?'

Jan explained why she had left Ellen at the castle and at once they all forgot about Duncan as they discussed the possibility of there being a wedding in the family before the summer was over.

Ellen and Andrew came soon after ten o'clock. One glance at their faces, dazed and slightly smiling, and Jan knew that they had solved their own particular problem and had come to some arrangement about their future together.

Sheena noticed too and she put down her knitting and without a word went over to them and kissed them both.

'It's taken the two of you long enough to make up your minds,' she rebuked them in her usual sharp manner, which was, after all, only a cloak for her real feelings. 'Are you not going to wish them well, John?'

'And why should I be doing that?' asked John, pretending in his teasing way that he did not understand what she was talking about.

'Because they are going to be married. I can see it in their faces,' murmured Agnes. 'Come here, Ellen, and let me kiss you.'

'Well, if *you* say it's in their faces it must be so,' said John, with a twinkle. 'I've never known you be wrong yet.'

Congratulations over, they began to discuss plans for the wedding, but it wasn't long before Sheena was telling them the news about Duncan being a writer.

'I thought there was something about him which didn't fit,' remarked Ellen. 'He's so knowledgeable about the theatre, for one thing. We've just dropped him at the end of the lane. We overtook him on the road from Dunmore to the ferry. He seemed a little shaken up, I thought, as if he'd had some bad news.'

'He told me he thinks that the poachers must have a car like Sandra Lang's and I asked him to keep a look-out for them,' said Andrew.

The conversation took a different turn and as she half-listened Jan felt a strange urgency rising within her to go to Tigh Uisdean and warn Duncan that by the next day, gossip being what it is, the whole glen would know that he was a writer and that he had deceived everyone by calling himself Duncan Davidson. If she didn't warn him he would think she had broken her promise to him, and she couldn't have him thinking that.

The feeling that she must go to him grew stronger with every minute. Although it was late she knew she wouldn't be able to rest unless she went. The others were so busy talking she did not think they would notice her leaving the room.

But as she rose from her chair her grandmother beckoned to her, so she went over to her and whispered to her, telling her where she was going and why. Agnes nodded understandingly and pressed her hand.

'Go with God, *mo chaileag*. The lad is needing you this night.'

Puzzled and a little afraid, as usual, of her grand-mother's ability to see what others failed to see, Jan slipped out through the back door into the mild air of the June night.

The sky was dark, blurred by hurrying clouds. Oc-casionally the moon appeared and lit up the countryside with the brilliance of a searchlight, silvering the walls of barns, striking diamond-bright sparks from the rough granite of the dykes, making long black shadows from trees and buildings stretch across the fields.

Through the farmyard gate she went on to the hill, on her way to Bealach Glas, the Green Gateway to Love, as her grandmother insisted on calling it. Ahead of her the mountain glittered faintly, then was lost as the moon dis-appeared behind another cloud. And it was like that all the way, bright light and darkness alternating, confusing the senses. A good night for poachers.

The new gate at Bealach Glas creaked a little as she opened it and swung back sharply into place. She skirted the potato field where the tops of the plants were thrust-ing above the surface of the soil. Who would harvest them? Would Duncan? Or would he leave now that it was known he wasn't Duncan Davidson?

The moon sailed out from behind a cloud and Jan had a brief glimpse of the white walls of the cottage. There was no light in the window to welcome her and she wondered if Duncan had gone to bed. As she approached the moon disappeared again and she felt that strange prickling down her back, the primitive warning of danger.

She stopped in her tracks and listened. There was a sound – an unusual one – a sort of scuffling ahead of her in the darkness. She moved towards it. Now she could hear the heavy breathing of an animal and occasional grunts accompanied the scuffling.

Moonlight shafted down brilliantly and there was the

animal in front of her, a monstrous thing with many legs and arms and three heads! Jan's hands went to her mouth to stifle a shriek.

It wasn't an animal. There on the path in front of the house were three men struggling, two of them trying to keep a third down. A new sound was added to the others, the sickening thuds of a booted foot kicking into flesh and bone. Fright and shock receded and another emotion took over driving her forward prepared to do battle.

'Stop it! Leave him alone!' she yelled.

The kicker whirled. He didn't wait to see who was yelling, but ran off towards the road shouting to the other man, who was picking himself up. He didn't wait either, but pounded off just as the moon slid behind another cloud.

'Wait!' cried Jan foolishly, and ran after them.

She was soon out of breath and she paused to fill her lungs she heard the sound of a car's engine starting up. Then it had gone, speeding down the road without lights.

Turning, Jan hurried back to the cottage garden, afraid of what she might find there. She could just make out a dim form sitting on the ground.

'Duncan, Duncan, are you all right? Wasn't I after telling you to be careful of them?'

She was on her knees in the earth not caring how she ruined the tights she had been wearing all that afternoon on account of her visit to the castle. She put her arms round him and held him close, searching his face with her fingers for signs of broken skin and finding it, feeling the blood sticky under her fingertips.

'They've hurt you!' she exclaimed. 'Can you stand up?'

He didn't answer and she realized that he was lying against her rather inertly. Had he lost consciousness? Fear because the poachers might have hit him on the back of the head with some weapon made her shake.

'Ach, Duncan, *mo chagar*,' she crooned, using in that

moment of stress the Gaelic endearment which her grandmother often used to her father and which meant simply 'my darling'. 'What have they done to you?'

'What did you say?' His voice was a little muffled because she was holding his head against her so closely, but the sound of it brought joy surging back.

'I asked what had they done to you?'

'Oh. I thought you said something else.'

Now he sounded normal, slightly amused as he pulled away from her and began to get to his feet. Once standing, he swayed a little, and she hurried to support him by holding his arm.

'Come into the house and sit down and I'll be tending to your wounds,' she said gently.

'Wounds?' he scoffed, freeing his arm from hers and walking towards the door and opening it. 'A couple of scratches and maybe a black eye, that's all. It's a pity you shouted out the way you did. If you'd had any sense you'd have kept quiet and gone back to the farm to fetch your father and Andrew. Between the three of us we could have got the measure of those two. Now they've got away and we'll probably never know who they are.'

He sounded irritated with her as he scraped a match alight and lit the lamp and she reacted badly.

'By the time I'd reached the farm and returned with Andrew and Father you'd have been finished off,' she retorted scornfully. 'Ach, have you no sense at all, taking on a couple of tinkers like that?'

In the glow of the lamplight she could see a cut on his right cheek which was bleeding profusely. Above the cut the right eye was beginning to swell. He removed his jacket, showing that his shirt was torn and one sleeve had almost been ripped out of its armhole. She longed to reach out and hold him in her arms again, but the derision in his eyes stopped her from taking any action.

'Look, mate,' he said, '*I* didn't take them on, *they* took me on. Oh, I knew they were somewhere about because that car, the one like Sandra's, was parked off the roadway. I came along the path quietly thinking I might surprise them. They were coming the other way and walked right into me. Being startled, they were aggressive.'

'I warned you that they wouldn't mind how they fought. Now will you please sit down and let me bathe your face. The blood is dripping down and making an awful mess of your shirt.'

He glanced down in surprise at the shirt, then grinned.

'Not much of a shirt left to make a mess of. I'll go and change it,' he murmured.

'Not until I've seen to that cut,' she declared, standing squarely in front of him. 'And looked at your eye. And felt your head. You nearly fainted in the garden and I wouldn't be at all surprised if you haven't got concussion, the daft way you're behaving!'

Duncan's eyes widened, but he didn't argue any more.

'All right, I'll sit down and you can play at being nurse. Funny how the sight of blood on a man's face brings out the Florence Nightingale in a woman.'

'Will you stop blethering and sit down,' she ordered crossly.

'Yes, nurse,' he replied with suspicious meekness, and sat down suddenly on the chair immediately behind him. Closing his eyes, he leaned his head against the top rung of the high ladderback of the chair. He had gone so pale he looked green.

Recalling the sound of those horrid thuds, worried about the possibility of internal injuries, Jan lit the new Primus stove and put on the kettle to boil water. In a cupboard she found first aid equipment. When the water had boiled she bathed the cut and applied ointment. Duncan kept his eyes closed and said nothing.

She couldn't do much about the black eye, so she felt the back of his head, her fingers searching amongst the

166

crisp black hair for a lump and finding one. There was no broken skin there.

'Take your shirt off,' she ordered, and he opened his eyes, pretending to look shocked.

'Now look here, nurse,' he began.

'Please, Duncan. I'm not being funny. You may have other cuts or bruises which need attention. One of those men kicked you, didn't he?'

'Yes,' he admitted, and reluctantly unbuttoned his shirt and took it off.

Lamplight gleamed on bare skin taut over big muscles and glinted on dark hairs which criss-crossed his chest. Trying to maintain a professional calm, Jan touched the two bruises which were showing at the bottom of the rib cage. He flinched but said nothing. She pressed harder.

'I don't think anything is broken or cracked. Can you breathe easily?' she asked, trying hard to remember what she had been taught about broken ribs.

'Not as well as usual,' he gasped, and she looked up sharply.

'What do you mean?' she asked shakily. Looking up had been a mistake. She had not realized how close she was to him.

'You took my breath away. Your hands are cold,' he replied with a grin.

Immediately she snatched her hands away and straightened up.

'Oh, I'm sorry,' she muttered. She had a feeling he was still mocking her. 'Where shall I find another shirt?' she asked stiffly.

'I'll get one,' he said, beginning to get out of the chair.

'No, you won't. You'll stay there until you've had a cup of tea. Now where's the shirt?'

'In the other room. In the chest of drawers. You'll have to take a candle.'

She found the shirt and when she returned Duncan was

still leaning back with his eyes closed. His colour was a little better, but not much, and she knew that he had taken a much worse beating than he was prepared to admit.

She helped him to put on the shirt and left him to button it while she made the tea. He still didn't possess a teapot, so it had to be a tinker's brew; and as she made it she recalled the first time she had drunk tea with him in that room.

She gave him his tea and sat down on a stool close to him.

'What brought you up here?' he asked. 'The second sight?'

'Yes, in a way it did, because Gran said you'd be needing me tonight. And Andrew mentioned that he'd asked you to look out for poachers and I . . .' She broke off, unable to tell him that she had been afraid for him because she loved him.

Loved him! The words danced flamelike in her mind. Since when had she loved him? Since that first time in this room when her spirit had recognized his and she hadn't wanted to leave the smoky firelit room and go out into the cold.

'You have the most exasperating trick of stopping in the middle of a sentence.' The deep voice was deriding her again. 'And just when you're about to say something interesting. I'm beginning to think you do it deliberately to keep me guessing, and while you pause you change your mind about what you're going to say. I'm sure your second thoughts aren't half as interesting as your first ones.'

Their eyes met. His seemed darker in the lamplight, and their expression was tantalizing.

'Come on, finish what you were going to say,' he urged softly.

'I was afraid,' she said weakly.

'For me?'

'Yes, I was afraid the poachers might hurt you.'

She looked away from him and took a sip of tea. It was still hot and she choked on it. A hand patted her on the back.

'Easy does it,' he mocked. His hand slid up to the nape of her neck and she felt his fingers in her thick hair. Involuntarily she stiffened, bracing herself against the longing to succumb to that gentle, seductive caress.

'Was that the only reason why you came?' he asked coolly, removing his fingers from her hair and leaning back in the chair again.

'No. I've something to tell you.'

In a rushed whisper she told him about the people who had arrived at the hotel and how everyone would soon know that he wasn't Duncan Davidson, odd job man, but David Garth, writer.

When she had finished he said a few succinct words about the people who had come and Jan turned wide shocked eyes on him.

He grinned at her unrepentantly.

'Roustabout language,' he said. 'It's all I can find to express my extreme irritation at the moment.'

'Have they come too soon? Haven't you finished the story?'

'In one way the story finished itself tonight at the castle, a fantastic ending which I couldn't have thought up even if I'd tried,' he said rather dourly. 'In fact ever since I left the castle I've been wandering about in a strange state not knowing what is real and what is fiction. The fight with those two poachers was most welcome. At least it felt *real*, every punch and kick of it.'

Jan stared at him anxiously, worried about concussion because he seemed to be talking wildly.

'What happened at the castle?' she asked.

'I made the most amazing discovery. I discovered that there's a very strong possibility that Sandra and I are cousins of sorts.'

'And hadn't that occurred to you before?'

'No. Why should it?' he countered.

'Some of us have been thinking that you've come to Glen Dearg because you knew that the MacClachan clan used to live here and you hoped to trace your relationship to them.'

'I'd never heard the name MacClachan until you mentioned it. I came here because the footsteps of that old sheep-shearer I knew once led to here. I promised I'd retrace them back across the world to Scotland.' He saw puzzlement on her face and added rather wearily, 'I see that I'll have to begin at the beginning.'

'Yes, please,' she whispered.

'Once upon a time,' he began, with a faint smile, 'there was a young woman called Helen Morton. She was a schoolteacher in a place called Cobarmulla. She met and became engaged to a young man called Tom Garth, who was the only son of a local pastoralist. One day when visiting their sheep station she met and fell violently in love with another young man who was possibly a roustabout working there. She ran away with him to Melbourne and married him.'

'Oh. Just like Fiona Duncan ran away with Hugh MacClachan,' exclaimed Jan.

'Yes, except that the outcome was more tragic, because they had not been married long when the young man was killed in an accident. Helen returned to Cobarmulla, and Tom Garth, still in love with her, welcomed her back, and married her.'

'And you were born and grew up thinking you were Tom Garth's son,' said Jan excitedly.

'I always said you're as sharp as a needle,' he teased. 'That's right, and he thought I was his son too. He brought me up to believe that one day I would inherit the sheep station and he trained me accordingly. But as time went on I found myself rebelling frequently and sometimes I even ran away into the bush.'

'Now I know why you know so much about sheep,' declared Jan.

'Right again, and also why I dislike the woolly things so much. I'd inherited my real father's wanderlust, I suppose. I wanted to travel and from my mother I'd inherited an interest in writing. I struggled and argued with Tom until he let me have my own way. And when I was seventeen I went off to Sydney and started to learn how to write the hard way, working for a newspaper. It was while I was there that my mother became ill. I rushed home to see her, almost too late. She had time to tell me that I wasn't Tom's son. She was going to tell me my real father's name and got as far as saying "Duncan Davids". I assumed she was going to say Davidson.'

'Did Tom Garth know you weren't his son?'

'Yes. She had told him to make him give in and let me follow my own choice of career. It was that more than anything else which swayed him and not my arguments as I'd thought. My mother left me a little money, the remains of her own inheritance, and with the knowledge that I owed nothing to Tom except my legal name and that my half-brother Bob was ideally suited to take over the sheep station when the time came, I was free to travel and write.'

'But where does the old sheep-shearer Davey come into the story?' asked Jan.

'He came with the usual band of sheep-shearers every year at clipping time. My mother always went out of her way to welcome him and he used to talk to me a lot. He told me how he'd always wanted to return to the Highlands, but had never been able to. He asked me to come in his place one day and I promised that I would.' He paused and the expression of regret which she had seen on his face once before when he'd spoken of the sheep-shearer crossed his face. 'After that he didn't come any more. I assumed that he'd grown too frail to work or had died. Taken up with my own struggle to assert myself, I pushed the promise to the back of my mind and almost forgot it. When I did eventually leave Australia to come to Britain it wasn't to fulfil the promise but to work on a documentary film about emigrants to Australia from this country.'

'What reminded you of the promise?'

'I suppose it was Phil Gibbons who I suspect is now at the hotel waiting to see me. He made the film about the emigrants and wanted to make another. I told him about Davey and he had this idea of approaching the story through the eyes of an Australian descendant of an emigrant re-tracing the footsteps of his ancestor back to Scotland. So I flew back to New South Wales and set off as an odd job man following Davey's path through Peru, California, British Columbia across Canada to Nova Scotia. It was a fascinating experience and I found plenty of material for the film.'

'How long has it taken you?'

'About two years, but in my mind I've been coming ever since I left Cobarmulla after my mother died, making a sort of subconscious pilgrimage. But I'd no idea that when I came to this glen it would involve me so personally. It was Phil who suggested that I change my name to come here. He thought there was a chance of someone here having heard of David Garth, script-writer.' His mouth twisted in a grin of self-mockery. 'I've often thought it was a precaution we needn't have taken, as was proved yesterday when you saw my real name and it meant nothing to you,' he added. 'I had every intention of leaving the glen before they started to film without any of you ever knowing why I'd come here, but obviously that plan has been ruined now.'

'Didn't you ever ask your mother's parents or family about your father's real name?' asked Jan curiously.

'No. There wasn't anyone to ask by the time I knew I wasn't Tom Garth's son.'

'She must have been going to say that your father was

Davey's son,' mused Jan. 'That would be why he took an interest in you and why he directed you to Glen Dearg. There are three other people besides my grandmother who are still alive and who remember Davey and think you resemble him.'

'Three?' he exclaimed, adding with a touch of derision. 'So you didn't give up looking for answers to your many questions?'

'No, and Colin has also guessed that there's possibly a connection between you and the MacClachans. He wanted to prove it so that you couldn't marry Sandra. You see, he's in love with her. He wasn't waiting for me to grow up. He was waiting for her to return to the glen, but when she returned you were here and got in his way.'

'How very inconsiderate of me,' he remarked dryly. 'I hope you and he have had the sense to keep all this about my likeness to a certain portrait to yourselves. The Colonel will be very annoyed with you if you've spread the information round the glen.'

'Why? What did he say to you? Did he show you the portrait? Oh, what did you think of it?' she demanded excitedly.

'I admit there is a likeness, but it isn't enough proof for me, nor is the picture of Gilbert Duncan and his daughter. However, Colonel Lang produced two letters, both from Davey MacClachan written to his grandfather Gilbert. One was from Nova Scotia saying that Hugh MacClachan had died there while working as a lumberjack. The other, dated several years later, was from Melbourne saying that Davey had a son whom he had called Duncan. He never wrote again, possibly because he never received a reply. The letters aren't really sufficient proof that I am Davey's grandson, but I have the Colonel worried and embarrassed. I told him my real reason for coming to the glen thinking to comfort him, but it didn't make him any happier. He gave me marching orders and said that on no account is the glen to be used in any film and that if the film company disregard his wishes he'll sue them. On that pleasant note we parted company and I came home without my supper,' said Duncan.

Jan sat silently, crouched on the stool, her fount of curiosity dried up. She guessed why the Colonel was worried and embarrassed by Duncan's presence in the glen. He feared that although Sandra and Duncan weren't first cousins they might be too closely related for marriage.

'It's late,' said Duncan suddenly. 'Time you went home.'

'Do you want me to go?' she challenged him.

'What I want has nothing to do with it,' he replied coolly. 'It's time you went home, and I'll walk with you to Bealach Glas to see you on your way and to make sure the fairies don't steal you.'

'You will not,' she retorted. 'You're not fit to go walking with a bump on your head like that. You're going to bed, and I'm going to sit here in the kitchen all night in case you get delirious and need nursing.'

'No.' He stood up tall and straight and glowered down at her, so Jan stood up too and faced him. 'You're going home now. I shan't get delirious and I won't need nursing.'

'Ach, I can see you don't trust me,' she replied. 'I'm really quite a good nurse. I just didn't stay to take the final examinations.'

'It's myself I don't trust,' he murmured enigmatically. 'Anyway, I'm not ill.'

'But you could be. Concussion is a strange thing. It has a way of . . .'

She couldn't go on because he had placed a hand over her mouth. She glared up at him and tried to wrench free of that gagging hand, but found she couldn't move because he had his other arm around her and was drawing her inexorably towards him. His hand slid from her mouth and under her chin. His mouth came down on hers and for a long time there was no more argument.

After a while Duncan said with a touch of laughter,

'Now you know why you daren't stay the night here!'

Jan leaned against him, breathless and helpless, listening to the beat of his heart and thinking in a vague muddled way of Fiona Duncan and Helen Morton, both of whom had loved so much that they had fled their comfortable homes and families to go with the men they loved. If those men had been like Duncan she could understand why.

'I could stay if only you would behave yourself,' she wheedled, but he put her from him and moved over to the door ready to open it.

'You're a stubborn child, like one of your own sheep when you set your mind on doing something,' he remarked.

'And you're stiff-necked, just like a . . . a MacClachan,' she retorted, annoyed with him because he'd called her a child. 'I'll go only if you promise to go to bed now and stay there until I come to see how you are in the morning.'

'I promise nothing,' he growled. 'Now go.'

He opened the door and, seeing that his face was set in unyielding lines, Jan offered no more opposition. He didn't want her company and he'd probably kissed her to punish her, hoping to frighten her away. He wasn't to know that instead of frightening her he had created a yearning within her for more of his kisses.

Distance was growing between them with every minute as he stood there tall and disdainful like the chieftain in the portrait. She could bear his coolness no longer so she went to the door and when it opened she ran out of the cottage without a word and didn't stop running until she reached Tighnacoarach.

She didn't sleep very well because she kept thinking that Duncan might leave without her seeing him again.

The feeling was so strong that she got up early and set off across the fields again to Bealach Glas. The morning was soft and still, promising heat later in the day. White mist lay thickly in hollows and wreathed itself round the summit of the mountain. Every blade of grass and every leaf was beaded with tiny silvery globules of moisture.

In the pale light of morning the cottage looked sleepy and smug. Blue-tits flitted amongst the bushes and swung acrobatically around the bird table Duncan had made for them. Going straight to the door, Jan lifted the latch and walked in. The room seemed the same. The two mugs she and Duncan had used were on the draining board by the sink. They'd been rinsed and left to drain. As she closed the door she realized that something was missing. The typewriter had gone from the table. The sheaf of type-written paper had gone too, although most of the books seemed to be there.

Quickly she stepped through the door which led to the other room. The bed was empty and had not been slept in. The rucksack had gone. The drawers in the chest were empty of clothing.

With a rising sense of desolation she returned to the other room and searched the table and the old stone mantelpiece for a note. There was none.

He had gone, leaving a few books, a renovated cottage and some ploughed and seeded fields as the only witness to his presence in the glen during the past few months.

Resisting a desire to sit down and weep, Jan closed the door and went back through the increasing warmth of the sunshine to the farmhouse. She hoped that her feeling of desolation didn't show, although she was aware that her mother was looking at her closely.

She went as usual to church and when the service was over and people lingered outside talking in the summer sunshine, she managed to get her sister Chris to herself for a few moments, away from the excited happy group which had collected around Ellen and Andrew to wish them well.

'Are the film people still at the hotel?' she asked as casually as she could.

'No. It's so disappointing,' sighed Chris. 'They left this morning soon after an early breakfast. Duncan arrived before six o'clock to see them and there seemed to be quite an argument going on. He left with them. They've decided not to use Glen Dearg in the film after all.' Chris glanced around saw the Colonel and Mrs. Lang talking to Ellen and Andrew and shielded her mouth with her hand as she muttered, 'I wouldn't be at all surprised if old Colonel Toffee-nose there has told them he didn't want *his* glen filmed. It would be just like him. He wouldn't be thinking of the rest of us and how we might benefit.'

'Did Duncan say he'd be coming back?'

'Not a word to me. I expect he's annoyed because he'd spent all that time here and now they're not going to use the place. Ach, there's Mrs. Campbell. I must have a word with her.'

Chris went off, not in the least concerned because Duncan had left the glen, and Jan turned to find Colin coming towards her.

'It's a fine day for a sail,' he said cheerfully. 'Would you like to come this afternoon?'

'He's gone,' she whispered. 'He left this morning.'

He knew at once whom she meant and showed no surprise.

'Is he coming back?'

'I don't think so.'

'What made him go?'

'Something the Colonel said to him.'

'I see.' Colin's eyes gleamed triumphantly. 'So he could be a MacClachan.'

'He says there's no real proof.'

'But there's enough to worry the Colonel,' guessed Colin shrewdly, 'and that's enough for me. What's all this about him being a writer? Seems you were right about

Davidson not being his name.'

Jan was just about to explain when Sandra came up to them.

'I hope you and Jan aren't planning to go sailing, Colin,' she said. 'I phoned you several times last evening to ask you to come and look at Perdita, but there was no reply. We're terribly worried about the poodle and Mummy wonders if you'd come over now to look at it. You could stay for lunch.'

Colin's eyes met Jan's. There was a hint of appeal in his expression. She nodded and he grinned gratefully.

'Yes, I can come,' he said to Sandra. 'Jan can't sail this afternoon. Perhaps you'd like to come out for an hour in the boat?'

'I'd love to,' replied Sandra enthusiastically. 'I'll go to the castle in your car, if you don't mind. The parents have a call to make on the way home. 'Bye, Jan. We'll be seeing you.'

Jan went home to Tighnacoarach where the main topic of discussion over Sunday dinner was, of course, the forthcoming wedding and where no one asked about Duncan. When eventually the rest of the family realized he had left the glen John regretted his going just when the clipping season was upon them and Sheena sighed over the loss of a bass to the choir.

In the following weeks Jan was glad of the hard work involved in clipping the sheep. It was one of the most social occasions in the life of the glen as each of the sheep farmers in the area took his turn at being host to all the other farmers and their farm workers when they came to help him clip his hundreds of sheep.

By the time the clipping was over full summer had clothed the glen in varying shades of green and the holiday season was in full swing. Choir practice had stopped for a while because Molly had gone away for her summer break. She would return at the end of August when there would be a series of concentrated rehearsals before they went off to the Mod. Between now and then a bass would have to be found to take Duncan's place.

Short of help on the farm after Duncan's departure John Reid decided to employ a student from an agricultural college, a cheerful young man called Peter Buchan who was willing and eager to learn all he could. Jan enjoyed working with him and even attended the Saturday evening dances held during the summer for the benefit of holidaymakers in the Legion Hall in his company.

After the wedding of Ellen and Andrew life settled down to its usual rhythm on the farm, but for the first time in her life Jan found herself restless and unsatisfied by the way of life in the glen. It did not take her long to find a reason for her restlessness. Her way of life had been disturbed by a stranger and now the place she loved was haunted by him. She found him everywhere. In the old shieling where she sheltered one day from a sudden squall, he leaned against the wall beside her and put his arm around her to keep her warm. Beside a drystone dyke he walked with her, and when they came to Bealach Glas he swung the gate shut between them and laughed at her as he leaned on the top bar.

The only person who mentioned him was her grandmother, who was perpetually asking her when Davey would be returning to the glen.

One day when Jan was shopping in Oban she ran into Sandra. The Colonel's daughter was dressed in neat navy blue trousers and a beautiful Fair Isle sweater and her gleaming hair was tied back in a ponytail. She was waiting, she said, for Colin. She was crewing for him in the sailing races being held as part of the regatta which was being held that week in Oban.

'Come and have a cup of coffee with me,' she suggested, and they went to the hotel on the Esplanade where Jan had lunched with Duncan and had danced with Colin, and which was headquarters of the yacht club during the regatta week. From the window of the dining-room they looked out on the many sailing yachts which had come from clubs all over the country to take part in the week of races. They were anchored off the esplanade and were tossing and turning on the wind-ruffed white-crested water of the bay.

'Do you ever hear anything from Duncan, or should I call him David?' asked Sandra.

'No. Do you?'

'No.' Sandra frowned at her coffee cup. 'It was so strange the way he left. After all my efforts to arrange a meeting for him with Daddy, he walked off that evening without a word, without even staying for supper. I've often wondered why.'

'Didn't your father tell you why?'

'Daddy can be terribly secretive. I just assumed when I heard about it that he didn't want the glen to be part of a film. I was disappointed too to find that Duncan had deceived us all about his name and his real reason for coming to the glen, but I was prepared to understand. For a while I was very attracted to him and thought he felt the same about me. Then he withdrew.' She frowned again and was silent as she puzzled over Duncan's behaviour. 'Anyway, it's over now,' she continued with her bright smile. 'Who knows, maybe Duncan's presence in the glen woke Colin up and made him notice me again. I'd better break the news to you while you're here. Colin and I are announcing our engagement this week, after the Regatta is over.'

'Congratulations,' muttered Jan, not really surprised.

'You don't mind?' Sandra had the grace to look anxious.

'Not at all. There was nothing serious between Colin and me. We're just friends, although I think he took me out in the spring in the hope of drawing your attention to him.'

Sandra laughed delightedly.

'It seems as if we were all at cross purposes in the spring. I must go now. I'm glad we've had this little talk. Wish us luck for the race today. If we win this one we'll probably get the trophy for the class.'

Jan wished her luck and went off to finish her shopping pondering on what Sandra had told her about Duncan's behaviour on the evening he should have stayed for supper at the castle. It looked as if Colonel Lang had decided to keep the possibility that Duncan might be related to the Lang family a secret, having extracted a promise from Duncan that he would leave the glen at once. Sandra had soon recovered from her infatuation for the stranger, and probably the Colonel and his wife had encouraged her friendship with Colin this time, instead of discouraging it, in order to help her forget Duncan.

But what of Duncan's feelings? And would she ever be able to think of him by his legal name of David? Or would he always be Duncan Davidson who had kissed her and had been welcome back again? Was he nursing a broken heart somewhere because he'd been unable to marry the red-haired heiress of his dreams? Or was he exulting in his freedom, having had another narrow escape from marriage which he regarded as a form of imprisonment?

One evening when July was hovering on the brink of August Jan vaulted the dry-stone dyke on to the road as she came off the hill. Dusk was gathering in the hollows of the hills and the land was sending up waves of warmth after a day of sunshine. Above the moor, which was tinted gold by the rays of the setting sun, a plover winged its lazy way home, and over the thick foliage of the trees she could see the loch shimmering with rose-shot light between the long dark ridges of land.

It was a scene of peaceful beauty, a setting for a tale of romance about knights and ladies and their troubadours, and possibly about shepherdesses and shepherds too.

Her romancing was interrupted by the scrunch of shoe-leather on the rough surface of the road. Someone was coming up the hill; someone who walked with a swing and a swagger and who was whistling as he came.

Jan stood frozen to the spot. Was she having hallucinations brought on by lingering on the hill too long and by indulging in vain imaginings? A sense of unreality enveloped her and she wished she could escape from it by running down to the hill home to the bright cheerfulness of the kitchen at the farmhouse and the homely chatter of her parents.

But she could not move, and as the whistler approached nearer looming large in the twilight her heart bounded with sheer joy as she recognized him. Recognition liberated her and she moved forward and said softly,

'Good evening. Have you come far?'

He stopped and his head jerked up in surprise. Eyes glimmered in a lean dark face as he peered down at her.

'Far enough,' he answered. 'Are you real?'

She laughed happily.

'Of course I am. Where are you going?'

'To Tigh Uisdean. I want to see if the potatoes are growing and if the oats are ripening.'

'But the bed isn't aired. You'd best come to the farm for the night.'

'No, thanks, I'll be fine.' He paused, peered down at her again and added, 'You could come with me if you like.'

Jan needed no second urging and, as shadows deepened and the cloak of night spread across the southern sky and a planet twinkled in the north-west, they walked up the road together, not speaking. Although Jan's tongue seemed to throb with the questions she longed to ask she kept quiet, allowing herself to enjoy the moments of silent union.

The door of the cottage opened easily. Duncan swung his rucksack to the floor and carried the portable typewriter in its case to the table, finding his way unerringly in the gloom. Jan stayed by the open door and waited.

A match scraped against the side of a box and its flame was reflected in the glass cover of the oil lamp. The cover was removed, the wick was turned up and the lighted match was set to it. The glow grew brighter as Duncan pumped the pressure up. In the soft light his profile was hawk-like and proud and his black hair sprang back vigorously from his forehead.

When the lamp was fully lit he turned and looked round the room. It was spick and span, shining and clean. There was a brightly-coloured rag rug on the floor in front of the hearth and a fire had been laid ready for lighting in the grate. On the two ladderback chairs bright cushions looked plump and soft. Even the old bench looked different because it had a padded seat. In front of the hearth some antique brass fire-irons winked and glittered in the lamplight.

Surprise chased across Duncan's face and he turned to look at Jan.

'Aren't you coming in?' he asked.

She closed the door and moved forward to sit on the bench.

'This place looks a lot cleaner and brighter since I left. Has someone been living in it?' he asked.

'I'd have told you if there had been,' she replied. 'I've been looking after it because I thought you might come back. Andrew said your rent was paid up to the end of September.'

'I'd really no intention of coming back,' he said. 'During the past six weeks I've done my best to forget Glen Dearg and all that happened here.' A wry grin twisted his mouth as he came across the room to sit on the bench beside her. 'But I couldn't forget. It kept popping up at the most surprising moments. I'd find myself wondering if the potatoes were growing and if the grain was ripening. Another time I'd feel a strong desire to see those twin lambs I helped to deliver and find out whether the weaker of the two has grown as strong as the other. I'd wonder about people, what they were doing and where they were going.'

He'd wondered about Sandra, thought Jan, feeling dejection set in.

'The potatoes are fine,' she said quickly. 'And the twin is easily as big as her sister. Has the film been made yet? The one you were writing the script for?'

'It's almost finished, I believe. They filmed it in another glen further north, just as beautiful and serving the purpose just as well.' He sounded indifferent as if he didn't care one way or the other about the film, and she supposed that was how it might be if you were a writer. Once a commission was finished you would forget it and turn your mind to the next one, as he had turned away from the glen and had tried to forget it.

But he had been unable to forget and he had come back. Why? Had he come for Sandra? Was history about to repeat itself?

'Has anything happened while I've been away?' he asked casually.

'Ellen and Andrew are married. I passed my proficiency test in clipping sheep. We have a student working on the farm. It's been a very good tourist season and . . .' She stopped, unable to tell him about Colin and Sandra.

'Here we go again,' he mocked. 'Stopping in the middle of a sentence. Come on, tell me what you were going to say.'

'You might not like it.'

'That's no reason why you shouldn't say it.'

'Duncan—' she began urgently.

'David,' he corrected her gently.

'Ach, I'll never be able to call you anything but Duncan.' she protested.

'We'll argue about that later,' he said. 'Now tell me

what you were going to say that I'm not going to like.'

'Very well. Sandra is going to marry Colin.'

There was a little silence. Jan glanced anxiously at him. To her surprise he was gazing at her and the expression in his eyes was as usual tantalizing, a little mocking. He didn't seem at all upset by the news.

'And why shouldn't I like that piece of news?' he asked lightly.

'I thought . . . you seemed . . . you and Sandra . . .' She stopped, saw his mouth quirk and flared, 'Ach, stop laughing at me! I thought you were in love with Sandra and went away because the Colonel said you couldn't marry her.'

'But I never wanted to marry her. Oh, I admit to being attracted to her, after all she has red hair, but as so often happens, when you think you've found your ideal she didn't measure up to other requirements,' he replied coolly. 'No, I didn't leave on account of Sandra – I left because the Colonel wouldn't allow the film to be made in the glen and we had to change our plans in a hurry.'

'You might have told me you were leaving.'

'How could I? If I remember rightly you ran out of the cottage without even saying good night,' he retorted. 'But you can now put it on record that Glen Dearg is the only place I've ever returned to.'

'That's because you belong here. The blood was strong and the heart was Highland,' she said softly.

'You can put it like that if it pleases your sentimental Highland heart,' he teased. 'But actually I have two very good reasons for returning.'

'What are they?' she asked curiously.

'One is to sing with the choir at the Mod, an experience which I don't think I should miss.'

She felt a little deflated by his answer, although in another way it pleased her because it meant Molly would not be let down and it also meant he would be here for at least another two months and she would be able to see him and possibly share some more happy moments with him.

'And the other reason?' she asked, fully expecting to be told that he wanted to harvest the potatoes and the barley and oats himself.

'That's not quite so easy to give,' he murmured. 'It depends, you see, on you.'

'On me?' she exclaimed.

'Yes. You've told me of two happy endings. Is there one in sight for you?'

Two happy endings. Ellen and Andrew. Colin and Sandra. He was asking her if she was going to be married. She stared at him trying to make sense out of what he had said by finding some clue in the expression on his face. He looked serious as if really interested in her reply.

A happy ending for herself. But she knew that there was no such thing as a happy ending. At one time she might have believed in it, but now she knew that there were only happy moments that had to be grasped while they happened; brief moments of joy which could support one for the rest of one's life; like this moment with him in the lamplit room of the old cottage; like the other moments she had known with him; like the moments she would know with him in the future. Happiness was in having them.

'I'm happy now,' she said simply.

'Why?'

'Because you're here. Because you've come back. Because you're going to stay at least until the end of September. I'm happy because we've been here before and in other places in the glen together, and even if you go away again I'll have had those moments with you.'

His eyes were dark in the lamplight, but the expression in them was no longer tantalizing or unreadable.

'You've grown up,' he murmured on a note of delight. 'and you've almost answered your own question. My other reason for returning the glen is this – I've wanted to be with you. You see, I also kept thinking of those moments we'd shared and when I'd been happy in the way I'm convinced we're all intended to be happy. I wanted to have more of them to store away in my mind so that when I'm not with you they'll pop up at unexpected times and I'll re-live them and I'll want to come back for more. I came back, Jan, because I love you.'

'Oh!' She was surprised. 'Then what are you going to do about it?'

'Kiss you and then ask you to marry me.'

He kissed her, and it took a long time. Then he asked her to marry him.

'Are you sure?' she asked cautiously. 'You won't think you're in prison?'

'Not if you'll let me go away occasionally on my travels.'

'Can I come with you sometimes?'

'If you like, but I thought you couldn't leave the glen.'

'I've been thinking about that a great deal since you left,' she admitted, 'and I've decided that I could leave it for someone I love very much.'

'Do you know someone you love very much?' he teased gently.

'I know and love you ...' She paused, saw his mouth twitch humorously and added quickly, 'David.'

Later, much later, when all the stars were twinkling in the cloudless night sky, they walked together by way of Bealach Glas to Tighnacoarach to tell the family that in future a married couple would be renting the croft known as Tigh Uisdean and that although they would often be away from the glen, they would always return to it when they were tired of travelling; to join in its life finding rest and refreshment in the rhythm and beauty of nature, returning because they both belonged there.

# Why the smile?

... because she has just received her **Free Harlequin Romance Catalogue!**

... and now she has a complete listing of the many, many Harlequin Romances still available.

... and now she can pick out titles by her favorite authors or fill in missing numbers for her library.

You too may have a **Free Harlequin Romance Catalogue** (and a smile!), simply by writing to:

## HARLEQUIN READER SERVICE

**DEPARTMENT C**
**M.P.O. BOX 707**
**NIAGARA FALLS N.Y.**
**14302**

*Canadian Address:*
**STRATFORD, ONTARIO**
**CANADA**

*Be sure to include your name and address!*

**Please Note:** Harlequin Romance Catalogue of available titles is revised every three months.

# BY POPULAR DEMAND

# 4 *Harlequin Presents...*

## EVERY MONTH

OVER THE YEARS many favourite Harlequin Romance authors have written novels which have not been available to Harlequin Romance. Now, because of the overwhelming response to Harlequin Presents, they are allowing us to publish these original works in the Harlequin Presents series. Authors such as Roberta Leigh, Rachel Lindsay, Rosalind Brett and Margaret Rome will be joining Anne Hampson, Anne Mather and Violet Winspear enabling us to publish 4 titles per month on a continuing basis.

*Look for these books at your local bookseller, or use the handy order coupon.* See title listing on following page.

---

**PLEASE NOTE:** All Harlequin Presents novels from #83 onwards are 95c. Books below that number, **where available** are priced at 75c through Harlequin Reader Service until December 31st, 1975.

---

To: HARLEQUIN READER SERVICE, Dept. N 504
   M.P.O. Box 707, Niagara Falls, N.Y. 14302
   Canadian address: Stratford, Ont., Canada

☐ Please send me the free Harlequin Romance Presents Catalogue.

☐ Please send me the titles checked on following page.

I enclose $ _____ (No C.O.D.'s). All books listed are 75c each. To help defray postage and handling cost, please add 25c.

Name _____

Address _____

City/Town _____

State/Prov. _____ Zip _____

# Have You Missed Any of These Harlequin Romances?

**PLEASE NOTE:** All Harlequin Romances from #1857 onwards are 75c. Books below that number, **where available** are priced at 60c through Harlequin Reader Service until December 31st, 1975.

# Have You Missed Any of These
# Harlequin Romances?